Also by Jan Springer

Pleasure Bound
A Hero's Welcome
A Hero Escapes
A Hero Betrayed
A Hero's Kiss
A Hero Wanted
Captive Heroes

Pleasure Bound Boxed Set
Pleasure Bound : COMPLETE SERIES SciFi Erotic Romance Boxed Set

Tentacles Shifter Erotic Romance
Taken by Him

The Key Club
A Merry Menage Christmas
Sophie's Menage
Jewel's Menage
Jaxie's Menage

The Outlaw Lovers
Jude Outlaw
The Claiming

Colter's Revenge
Tyler's Woman
Resistance
The Outlaw Lovers
Alpha Outlaws Boxed Set

Vampira
Sweet Heat
Dark Heat
Wet Heat
Crimson Heat

Standalone
A Touch of Menage Boxed Set
Shades of Menage Boxed Set
Nice Girl Naughty
Sinderella Sexy
The Biker and The Bride
The Fire Within
Bared to Him
Pleasure Bound : A Futuristic Adult Romance Boxed Set
Merry Menage Kisses Boxed Set
Inner Girl Rising
Stripped Naked
Risqué Girl Delights Boxed Set
A Holiday Menage
Ménage À Trois
A Hitman for Hannah
Billionaire Boyfriend
Edible Delights

Vampira
Toygasm
The Dark Side

Watch for more at www.janspringer.com.

A HERO WANTED
Pleasure Bound Book Five
(Loosely connected with the Pleasure Bound series)
Jan Springer

Old-fashioned gal needs a man who loves to walk in the rain. Must be well-hung. A homebody, white picket fence-type of guy. Sexual requirements-gentle yet untamed lover. He must be sexually adventurous who will train me to be same. Must be romantic, enjoy toys, interested in mutual light bondage, ménages are welcome.

That's what full-figured, antiques shop owner Jenna MacLean wants when she and her best friend outline a want ad just for fun on their weekly girls' night out.

After years of being away from his pretty-plus sized ex-girlfriend, Sully's back in town. When he finds the want ad, he knows he's the only man who can make all of Jenna's sizzling-hot fantasies come true.

She's never left his heart and he needs her back in his bed-but he's not going the traditional romantic route. This time, he'll prove he loves her with help from the notorious Ménage Club, a relationship club designed specifically to get estranged couples back together with the help of a third and sometimes a fourth in the bedroom.

1

A Hero Wanted is loosely connected with the Pleasure Bound Series.

A Hero Wanted is Book 5
It takes place on Earth...the other stories in the series take place on the recently discovered mysterious planet, Paradise...
Please note there are boxed sets available for this series.
Save $ and get
Pleasure Bound ~ The Complete Series 1- 6 Box Set
or
Pleasure Bound 1-5 Box Set and 6 separately.
Enjoy!

A Hero Wanted
Published by Spunky Girl Publishing
Copyright 2015 by Jan Springer
Discover other titles by Jan Springer at http:www.janspringer.com[1]
Cover Art by Talina Perkins ~ Bookin' It Designs
Edited by Amelia S. Black
License Notes

Creative Note

---

1. http://www.janspringer.com

JAN'S NEWSLETTER

Hi! If you would like to get an email when my books are released, you can sign up here:

Newsletter: http://ymlp.com/xguembmugmgb

Your emails will never be shared and you can unsubscribe whenever you like.

Chapter One

In the not too distant future...

Jenna MacLean trembled with excitement as her ex-boyfriend Sully Hero sauntered toward where she sat on her lace-canopied, four-poster bed. His six-foot, naked, muscular body appeared tense and his huge cock was fully engorged, ready to impale her.

Behind him she spotted another man silhouetted against the rose-patterned wallpaper watching her. His features were blurry, his identity not yet recognizable But she knew the other man would be just as well-hung, just as eager to please her.

Oh, yes! Come to me!

Reaching between her legs, she found her ultra-sensitive clit and massaged it, allowing both men to watch.

Sexy sparks of need flashed through Sully's green gaze and his cock blushed a deep shade of purple—his smooth, mushroom-shaped cock head looked angry and just as purple as it thrust itself from its sheath.

She could smell him. An erotic masculine scent that played havoc with her senses. Made her crave the wicked pleasures he gave so willingly.

Heavy, tortured breaths shot through the air as he stood over her bed, his hand stroking the massive eight-inch length of his silk-encased cock.

Stroking. Touching. Preparing.

Oh! She'd craved to have Sully back in her life for so long.

Her breathing quickened, met his in the same wicked quick tempo. His erection seemed so unbelievably long. Longer than she remembered. Thick as sin. Ready to pleasure her.

Her finger moved frantically over her slippery, achy clit, Erotic pleasure spiraled around her, making her whimper and squirm as both men watched.

Desperate hunger blazed across Sully's handsome face. The sight made her cry out her own want.

"I let you get away from me too many times, Jenna," he growled. "It won't happen again. Once you've been initiated into the Ménage Club you'll never leave me." The passion searing his voice made her believe he would stay with her forever. Never leave her again.

His mention of the notorious Ménage Club made shivers of delight shoot through her. The club specialized in bringing couples back together, couples who would otherwise never do so on their own. Couples like Sully and her.

Sully and the man in the background moved closer. Moved toward her like wild predators surrounding their mate. Each ready to take her.

Muscles in their broad chests rippled, tanned muscles in their arms bulged as they both continued to rub their engorged cocks.

The mattress shifted beneath her as the two men came upon her bed.

Her breath quickened. She'd waited so long for this. Waited too long!

"Okay, what else should I put down in the want ad?"

Jenna MacLean blinked herself out of the fantasy and found her best friend, twenty-five-year-old Meemee Caldwell, staring at her with blue-gray eyes that glittered with such excitement Jenna had to force herself to steady her breath as she focused her attention back to the white napkin set on the table in front of them.

"What have we got so far?" Jenna asked, trying hard to ignore how husky her voice sounded.

Meemee grimaced. Her wine-colored lips dipped into a frown and her straight golden-colored blonde hair swung over her shoulders as she looked down at the napkin she'd been using to write Jenna's boyfriend wanted ad.

"'A Hero Wanted. White picket fence type gal wants a man who loves to walk in the rain.' What else?" Meemee said.

"Okay... I want him to have a nice sense of humor. Must be gentle and caring. Also white picket fence material."

Meemee rolled her eyes, opened her mouth, pretended to stick her finger down her throat and made a gagging sound. "Oh, come on. If you want humor, gentle and caring, and a fenced yard, get yourself a Saint Bernard dog."

Jenna giggled. "Don't take it so seriously, Meems. We're only pretending."

"Me? Serious? Oh, please. Never. You know me better than that. I am the last person on this earth who'd take anything serious. I'm just curious about what kind of guy would rip your soul apart. What kind of man makes your heart pound? Your legs weaken? Makes your pussy scream for his cock. Oh, shit, I forgot to write down he has to be well-hung. He has to have the tool to do the job, am I right?"

Definitely well-hung. Jenna nodded in agreement as Meemee began writing again.

"And make his cock at least eight inches long, two inches thick."

"Now you're talking, Jen. Give me more. Give me your *heart*."

Meemee gazed at her with such sweet desperation that it made Jenna a bit uneasy. Meems was definitely looking at this too seriously. But what the heck did it matter? No one would see it. It was just something to pass the time, something to giggle over on their weekly girls' night out.

"So? What do you want in a man, Jen? Spill it."

"I want..." Gosh, what did she want?

She looked around the cozy western-themed room. It was decorated with several large wagon wheels on the ceiling, rough-hewn, pine-planked walls and tiny, flickering oil lamps set in the middle of white and red checkered cloth-covered square tables. A rustic red-bricked fireplace complete with a black cauldron hung over flickering blue-yellow flames. Nestled in a corner, totally out of its element sat a Fifties-style jukebox, blasting out a Shania Twain tune.

Jenna's mouth watered at the tantalizing scents of frying burgers and baking pepperoni pizza. She focused her attention to the two sexy bartenders pouring drinks behind the nearby mahogany bar—in particular to the tall, muscular, brown-haired hunk.

A familiar yearning started deep down in her lower belly.

She wanted *him*. She wanted Sully Well-Hung Hero. But he was off-limits. He'd made his decision about their relationship when he'd walked out on them over four years ago to join NASA's newly formed Hyperspace program. Despite the fact that he had abandoned her, she just couldn't stop herself from coming to his damn bar and getting her eye-candy fix of him every week since he'd come back to town.

Wow, did she have a problem with torturing herself or what?

"Green eyes," she mumbled as she kept an eye on Sully.

The son of a bitch appeared to be flirting with some perfectly thin, leggy, blonde bitch as he poured her a drink from behind the bar. The blonde laughed at something he said and her irritating voice grated along Jenna's nerves, making that familiar, awful jealousy she hated so much spring through her like a heated torch.

He'd been back in town for a month and hadn't so much as taken the time to say anything more than a formal hello whenever she and Meems came into his newly purchased bar on their weekly jaunt. Not that she expected him to say much to her. Especially after the way they'd left things in the past.

"And he should be clean-cut, have dark brown, short hair...a homebody...maybe a guy who looks like Orlando Bloom." Or Sully. "But he has to be a guy who wants to settle down."

Somebody totally the opposite of Sully.

Maybe she should find a guy not as good-looking as him. A guy who didn't capture every red-blooded woman's attention whenever he passed them on the street. The attention he got from gorgeously sexy women made her feel as if she were not good enough for him simply because he was physically fit and she wasn't.

Her pulse quickened at the sight of Sully's shoulder muscles rippling beneath the tight, black, muscle T-shirt that said in bold, white lettering across his wide chest *Sully's Bar & Grill*.

She could still remember how hard those tanned muscles felt beneath her exploring fingertips when they'd made love. How his groans of arousal had made her feel so powerful. Had made her blush as her insecurities about being too overweight to attract such a gorgeous hunk always seemed to blossom whenever she'd been naked with him.

"Okay, so I gather you're stuck about what to put down. How about sexually? Do you want sex gentle or untamed with your man?"

"Depends on our mood. One thing for sure is I want him sexually adventurous so he can teach me to be the same way," Jenna replied, ripping her gaze from Sully and back to her friend.

"Sexually adventurous trainer wanted." Her friend nodded her approval as she wrote it down on the napkin.

Oh, why couldn't she look more like Meems? Meemee was curvy, svelte, blonde and so very pretty with her big blue eyes and a gorgeous body that attracted delicious-looking hunks who seemed to flutter around her like butterflies. Hunks she used to satisfy herself with sexually and then casually tossed aside.

Although Meemee had never told her, Jenna suspected her friend had the hots for Tony, their lifelong friend and Sully's part-time bartender and best friend.

Tony's sharp angular features, short, feathery black hair and bronzed skin didn't betray his Greek heritage. He was also the man who had created and owned the Ménage Club. It wasn't just a swinger's club where men and women ventured to for sex. It was a relationship club. A place where couples could face their worst fears, and Jenna knew she had some issues she wouldn't mind working on.

Gosh! They were both so pathetic in drooling over men they couldn't have. Try as they might not to venture into Sully's bar, one or the other always mentioned it after they'd seen their weekly movie or after a shopping spree. "And he has to be romantic. Sex toys would be nice too. He's got to like sex toys."

"Sex toys. Now you're talking, woman," Meemee giggled, and kept writing, leaving Jenna to remember the first time Sully had mentioned they should try toys to allow them to enjoy sex in a different, exciting way. Back then, though, she'd been unable to accept them as a natural part of their relationship. She'd been so inexperienced. Insecure and no confidence in herself as a woman. Back then she hadn't been able to understand how Sully had even been attracted to her with her size eighteen, sometimes twenty, sometimes sixteen-sized body.

She'd had big breasts, a wide waist and a nice big butt. Yet he'd pursued her. She'd been twenty and he'd been twenty-one. Sully had been her first lover and after their breakup, he hadn't been her last. She'd slept with two more guys. Guys she'd cared about. They just hadn't been as passionate in bed or as tender as Sully.

Jenna sighed.

Saying no to sex toys with Sully had been a big mistake. It had been an even bigger slip-up letting him go so easily. But back then she'd adopted her grandmother's frame of mind that a couple in love didn't need arousal by artificial stimulation. That their bodies should have been enough to keep each other satisfied. On top of that, his mention of sex toys had made her feel insecure about her sexuality. Made her think if she was truly satisfying him in bed, as he'd said, he wouldn't be thinking of other ways to get aroused.

As she'd grown older though, her craving to have Sully back had changed her tastes and her beliefs. She'd begun to realize she'd taken on her grandmother's excess baggage where sex was concerned. She'd stifled her own natural need to explore her sexuality.

Now that her grandparents were dead and she was finally out from under their overly strict rules and living on her own, Jenna felt more open to new ideas about sex. Okay, so she was a lot more open to sex and what it stood for in a loving relationship.

"And he's got to be into anal play," Jenna whispered, trying out the new territory on her friend. To her surprise, Meemee held a straight face as she kept pen to napkin.

"And he has to be interested in light bondage."

Meemee looked up with a curious glint in her eyes. She remained serious.

"Meaning he has to like it on himself? Or on you?"

"Both of us."

Meems nodded. "Nice. Very nice. Hero has to be into mutual light bondage."

"Definitely ménages...to keep the sex life spicy," Jenna continued as her thoughts flew back to the exclusive Ménage Club. Indiscreet research through friends had revealed the secret club consisted of a group of men and women who swore troubled couples could get together again with the help of a third.

"Ménages are welcome," Meemee said as she wrote quickly. "What else?"

Jenna sighed and tried to put Sully out of her mind. It didn't work. They'd fought much too often during their relationship. Broken up more times than she could count and now, years later, she was more than willing to join the Club. She wanted to watch the enjoyment flash across his face and watch his cock harden while another man pleasured her. She was willing to use the Club to patch things up between them and face her jealousies and insecurities. Unfortunately, now that her interest in sex had finally broken free, he'd lost interest in her.

She sighed and frowned as disappointment worked its way through her. "That's about it. But at the top of the list he definitely has to be a white picket fence kind of guy."

Meaning a man who wouldn't run out on her no matter how badly they fought. A man who wouldn't walk away no matter how many times he said he loved her. A man so unlike Sully.

"He sounds absolutely delicious," Meemee cooed. "Not many of those types around town these days."

"Can I get you two ladies anything else?"

Sully Hero's deep voice sailed through the air and gripped Jenna, heating her pussy so wickedly, she almost moaned aloud. God help her, she always reacted so deliciously toward his masculine voice, even after all this time apart.

"I'd like another beer, Sully." Meemee grinned. "And please don't call us ladies. There are no ladies in this booth."

Sully's intense green gaze zeroed in on Jenna. "You sure about that?"

Jenna got his meaning loud and clear. As far as he was concerned, she was a pure lady, no wildcat in her.

"So, Sully," Meems said apparently noticing the tension burning through the air. "Take a look at this ad Jen and I are working on. Give us a man's opinion. If you saw it in the newspaper, would you answer it?"

Horrified, Jenna helplessly watched as Meemee, with a sly grin plastered across her face, handed Sully the napkin with the ad on it.

Meems had set her up! Bitch!

"A Hero Wanted," Sully read, and cocked an eyebrow at Jenna.

"Jenna came up with that one."

"She did, did she?" His hot look rammed her and ripped her breath away.

"Actually, the ad is hers," Meemee admitted, and winked at Jenna.

Satisfied pleasure zipped through her as his eyes widened. Obviously he was shocked at what Meemee had written for her, proving yet again his opinion about her being straightlaced hadn't changed.

"The ad is private. If you wouldn't mind..." Jenna said coolly and held out her hand, expecting him to give the napkin back, but he ignored her and kept reading.

"White picket fence-type, old-fashioned gal needs a man who loves to walk in the rain..." He continued on in silence then cleared his throat, and said in a somewhat strangled voice, "Must be well-hung. Eight inches at least."

Oh, heavens! Was this embarrassing or what? Was he remembering the one time she'd mustered up the courage to measure Sully's cock just for fun? He'd been exactly eight glorious inches long and two inches thick.

She threw Meemee a hateful glance. A look that promised her best friend she was in big trouble. Meemee, however, seemed unfazed and smiled.

Damn her!

"Sex toys, huh?" Interest tinged Sully's voice.

Heat sparked her cheeks and curled like wildfire through her from tip to toes.

Oh, boy, it was getting too hot in here. She needed another beer. An ice-cold one. A frozen one would be even better. Then she could roll the frosty bottle over her suddenly too-tight breasts and aching nipples. Not to mention sliding it against her suddenly feverish pussy.

But until that could happen, she'd settle for grabbing her ice water glass and resting it against her flaming cheeks. She eyed the glass on the table and the delicious-looking, half-melted ice cubes floating around at the top, resisting the urge to dip her finger inside, grab a cube and run it between her hot pussy lips.

"Someone to teach you to be sexually adventurous?"

There was that tinge of surprise in his voice again. A sudden inhalation of his breath as he continued. "Romance, light bondage, anal..."

He stopped—obviously he was reading the "ménages are welcome" part.

Would he think she was being too promiscuous by mentioning all those things? Or would he take the hint that she was now interested in being with him and willing to join the Ménage Club to fix their nonexistent relationship?

Her face grew hotter.

"So? What do you think, Sully?" Meemee asked, thankfully coming to her rescue. The tone of her voice sounded so sweetly innocent, as if she hadn't set the whole thing up.

"I'm sure there would be lots of guys answering this type of ad," Sully replied, and placed the napkin in front of Jenna. She didn't hesitate to snap it up and crunch it in her hand, hiding it from his smoldering gaze.

"You sound like every guy's wet-dream girl...but can you deliver if someone answers the ad?" he asked.

His bold question made her stiffen in her seat. The son of a bitch had just insulted her by insinuating she wouldn't deliver.

She forced herself to relax. Sully had no intention of answering her ad—he was too busy flirting with his big-boobed, leggy, blonde bitch clients at the bar.

"Oh, I'm sure whoever answers my ad will be quite satisfied," Jenna purred, enjoying the wild spark flaring in his eyes. "It's just too bad my hero hasn't come along yet. He's missing out on a lot."

"Perhaps," Meemee broke in softly as she thoughtfully fingered the mouth of her almost empty beer bottle, "her hero is standing right beneath her nose and she doesn't even know it yet?"

Good one, Meems. She threw Meemee another hateful glance. The last complication she needed in her life was sexy Sully Hero. He would have her in his bed twenty-four/seven just as he'd tried to do years ago. Not that she would necessarily mind this time around. This time she didn't have her overly protective grandparents waiting for her to come home. They'd always asked her where she'd been and what she'd been doing. Her relationship with her grandparents hadn't been an open one about sex, so she'd always lied and said she'd been out with Meemee. Although she'd been twenty at the time when she'd met Sully, she'd still been living with her grandparents and feeling it was her duty to help her grandmother take care of her grandfather after he'd suffered a devastating stroke several years prior.

Now as he stood beside the table, she eagerly awaiting his answer. None came as a pretty, long-legged blonde waitress suddenly interrupted them.

God! What was it with Sully and all these blonde women?

"Boss, the cook is threatening to quit again," she said in a flirty voice.

Sully looked as if he might say something to Jenna and she held her breath, anxiously waiting like a pathetic dog for him to give her a glimmer of hope that they just might have another chance. Instead, he simply nodded and left with the waitress.

Meemee slapped her hands onto the table in front of her and shook her head with wonder at her.

"Shit, Jenna. He is so fucking hot! Why did you let him go?"

"Meems, please, I already told you why we split up."

"Yeah, I know you said it was all those fights you two had. For instance, *your* hang-up about your weight—*your* insane jealousy about other women who looked at him—*your* inability to enjoy sex without feeling a tad guilty whenever he wanted to try anything but the missionary position. But Sully came back *here*, Jenna, after saying he'd never come back. And he even bought the bar. Maybe he came back for you?"

"You're dreaming, Meems. He didn't come back for me."

If he had, he would have approached her by now. Wouldn't he?

"Then why would he come back here of all places? Why return to the one place he swore he'd never come back to when you two broke up?"

She'd been thinking about that herself. "I'm sure his reasons are personal."

"Meaning?"

"I mean it is none of our business why he came back here, understand?"

"Loud and clear." Meemee grinned wickedly. She sucked back the last of her beer, leaving Jenna with the idea her friend had something else up her sleeve. Something she wasn't going to like.

A HERO WANTED

White picket fence-type, old-fashioned gal needs a man who loves to walk in the rain. Must be well-hung. At least eight inches long. Two inches thick. Sharp green eyes. Clean-cut. Dark brown, short hair...a homebody, white picket fence type of guy.

Sexual requirements—gentle yet untamed lover. Sexually adventurous who will train to be same.

Must be romantic, enjoy sex toys, into anal play, interested in mutual light bondage, ménages are welcome.

Sully lifted the crinkled napkin off the night table from where he'd left it before taking his cold shower and pressed it against his nostrils, inhaling Jenna's sweet, seductive scent. His heart picked up speed and his shaft hardened with exquisite need.

Christ! Her feminine aroma always did that to him. Always made his mind whirl out of control, made him want to tangle his fingers through her luscious hair, made him want to stare into her bright blue, sparkling eyes that reminded him of storm clouds every time they'd fought—and they'd fought a lot.

Nonetheless he'd never gotten enough of staring into her eyes. Never got tired of stroking his hands along her voluptuous, silky, plus-size curves and sinking his fingers into her fleshy hips when he thrust his cock into her tight pussy.

She made him want to explore her every curvy crevice. Taste every part of her. Tonight at the bar he'd watched her perfectly shaped eyebrows arch with irritation as he'd read her Hero Wanted ad. He'd wanted to grab her, tug her upstairs, throw her on his bed and lose himself inside her tight pussy. Just as he'd been able to do in the past.

Being away from her had been hell. He'd found that fact out shortly after he'd left her.

Even with NASA inventing spaceships that could use small amounts of hydrogen to fuel rockets into exploring space, allowing him to travel extensively throughout the galaxy and do what he'd always dreamed of doing, he'd missed her. The new, safe rockets as well as the invention of hyperspace travel had made it easy for NASA to put out the call for men and women who were interested in space exploration to join the NASA team of astronauts. Training was minimal, training pay fantastic and the computers took care of everything on the spaceships. All he had to do was make sure the cameras recorded everywhere he went on the planets.

Although training was exciting and the subsequent contract of space exploration had been intriguing, he hadn't been able to get Jenna MacLean out of his mind. He'd barely gotten through the past four years without wanting to pick up the phone every day and talk to her and tell her he still loved her but, of course, that had been out of the question. They'd broken up and the last things they'd said to each other hadn't been pretty.

Recently, when a plum, top secret NASA assignment to explore the newly discovered planet named Paradise using a highly specialized warp speed, hydrogen spaceship was dropped in his and his cousins' laps, he'd backed out at the last minute—backing out and coming back to Hideaway to plunge his entire life savings into this bar and secure the assistance of Tony and his Ménage Club to help him get Jenna back.

He blew out a frustrated breath as he drew the scented napkin away from his face and once again read the scribbled words.

The physical description on the ad was definitely him, but what about the rest? Had the two women simply been goofing around? Or had Jenna left it on the booth table for him to find on purpose? Or maybe she'd simply forgotten to take it along with her after the girls had left?

Jenna wanted a white picket fence kind of guy. By purchasing this bar and preparing the apartment upstairs, would she consider him white picket fence material? Would she ever trust him not to leave her again? He'd seen the pain, the hurt in her eyes every time she looked at him.

The mistrust made his gut twist in agony. So much so, he couldn't even bring himself to apologize to her.

Could he trust himself not to impulsively take off again if things didn't work out between them? Jenna had a jealousy streak that had made them fight like cats and dogs. He knew it stemmed from her insecurity of being overweight and the fact that he had tons of women who were his friends. But that's all they were—friends.

She hadn't been able to get used to the idea that he wanted *her*. Only her. No matter how many times he'd told her he'd always been physically attracted to plus-size women, the green-eyed monster of jealousy had just sat between them.

He'd watched Jenna tonight. Snuck peeks at her as one of the women from the Club had flirted with him. He'd seen the way Jenna's blue eyes had sparked with that familiar anger when she'd looked his way. Obviously her jealousy hadn't changed. If they got back together, it would only be a matter of time before they were fighting again. It would just be the same old song and dance. Fights just weren't his cup of tea.

One thing he knew for sure though, he wanted Jenna with his very heart and soul.

One thing he didn't know for sure was had he done the right thing in asking for help from the Ménage Club without asking her first?

He eyed the phone and resisted the impulse to pick up the receiver, call her and ask if she was still as interested in him as he was in her.

Maybe he should just throw the want ad napkin away? Maybe he should just sell the bar and get the hell out of town?

Maybe he should just go and take another cold shower.

"DAMMIT! WHERE IS THAT napkin?" Jenna hissed as she rummaged through her bag after she'd plopped it onto the bathroom counter when she'd returned home. She was sure she'd dumped the napkin into a side pocket of her purse right after Sully had left the booth. But now it wasn't there.

Shit!

Unfortunately, the remnants of his heated looks were still playing tease with her. Her nipples ached to be touched and her clit needed to be soothed desperately—all because of Sully Hero.

Why in the world had he come back here and not gone off to God knew where with his astronaut cousins? And why did she insist on going to Sully's bar every Friday night and submitting herself to this torturous, sexual hell every time she came home without him?

That son of a bitch! He was probably screwing the blonde bombshell who'd been flirting with him. Just the thought of him being in another woman's arms made that familiar roar of red-hot anger grip her.

Oh! She hated feeling this way. Hated the idea that Sully might prefer a skinny chick over her. Hated the idea that she still cared about him at all.

Looking at herself in the mirror, she slipped off her blouse, unlatched the front clasps on her bra and watched her generous 36D-sized breasts fall free. Her globes looked heavy and swollen, her large, pink, lollipop-sized nipples appeared taut beneath the glare of her bathroom lights.

Damn Sully Hero for making her react this way every time he was in the same room as her.

Glancing lower, she noticed her thick waistline bulging slightly over her size sixteen skirt.

She frowned. Okay so she was still as overweight as ever. It wasn't as if she hadn't tried to slim down a little. She ate relatively well, exercised almost every day with brisk, early morning walks and yet she never lost weight.

Her grandmother said it was in their genes. MacLean women were good farm stock material. Always on the big side. Big-boned, big-boobed and big-assed.

Even her grandmother had been overweight all her life, and pictures of her late mom showed her being overweight too.

When Jenna had been younger, she'd tried to defy her heritage, gone the diet route, laxatives, played a little with the bulimia stuff and tried to shed her pounds that way, but all it had gotten her in the end was sick as a dog.

She'd finally accepted herself as being a plus-size woman. Destined to be a size eighteen, sometimes size twenty, sometimes size sixteen, bouncing between a hundred and sixty and a hundred and ninety pounds for the rest of her life. She'd thought she'd gotten used to the idea, thought she'd finally felt comfortable in her own skin, that is...until sexy, well-hung Sully had sauntered back into town and conjured up all her insecurities again. Stupid, immature insecurities that whispered to her he was just too good-looking for tubby her.

Frig!

Why should she even care that he talked to other women more than he did to her? Their relationship was in the past, but those intense sexual sensations she got whenever she was around him or smelled him wasn't history. Those feelings were alive and eating her up—making her feel like a firecracker about to explode.

Frowning, she reached into a nearby drawer and pulled out the weighted nipple clamps she'd ordered through her favorite sex toy Internet site. According to the site, these clamps were made for beginners, the tension being adjustable and the grips rubber-tipped. She'd worked her way up to wearing them at tighter and longer tension levels until she now craved a harder grip. But these would do until she could get online and search for new ones.

She inhaled softly as each clamp bit into her tender, aroused nipples. She allowed the foot-long chain with the crystal stone weight to dangle between her breasts. The sight of her breasts being decorated in this way turned her on, adding to the already lusty feelings roaring through her at the thought of Sully being there in the bathroom with her, watching her, wanting her.

Ignoring the painful pleasure-pinch of the clamps, she unzipped her skirt and let it fall to the ceramic floor with a soft rustle, then pulled down her thong underwear and stepped out of them. From the same drawer she withdrew the glass dildo wand she'd bought at the same time as the clamps.

Dubbed the Long Dong Torpedo, it consisted of a nontoxic, red liquid glycerin compound that generated unbelievable heat just as a man's cock did. Eight inches long and two inches wide, it fit inside her pussy nice and snuggly, just as Sully's penis once had.

Slipping her free hand between her widespread legs, Jenna bit her lip to keep from crying out as her finger eagerly pushed past her swollen pussy lips and slipped inside her vagina to collect some moisture. Gliding back out she then began a slow, erotic slide of her wet finger over her aching clit while watching her reactions in the mirror.

This is what Sully would see when he watched another man touch her.

Half-lidded eyes, her full, red lips slightly parted as the increasing aroused bliss blew around her, her pink nipples growing darker beneath the sharp pinch of the clamps.

At the beginning, when she'd first started playing with the clamps, she'd kept them on only for five to ten minutes at a time, allowing herself to get used to the pleasure-pain, allowing her nipples to receive its much-needed blood supply. But now, she'd graduated and could keep them on for up to thirty minutes inside her comfort zone of pleasure-pain.

Her clit pulsed and sent shimmers of delight outward as she feverishly moved her wet finger over her swollen, tender flesh.

In the mirror, she watched the length of silvery chain sway between her breasts as she inhaled harshly, the heavy stone hanging from the middle of the chain trying to drag her nipples down.

Would Sully enjoy watching the pleasure skim across her face as another man ran his finger over her engorged clit, making her moan and whimper?

Jenna drew more moisture from her ever increasingly wet vagina and rubbed harder, faster. She could feel the familiar sexual tension grip her. Could see her eyes begin to close. Heard her breathing grow heavy and tortured as her want for pleasure increased.

Grabbing the huge glass wand, she imagined it to be Sully's hot cock as she plunged it into her vagina in one quick thrust, burying it into her wetness.

Oh, yes! So hot! So big!

Keeping both hands moving, one finger eagerly rubbing her clit, the other sliding the dildo in and out of her, she scrunched her eyes tight and allowed the pleasure to burst over her.

Within seconds she became lost in the frantic, erotic waves of bliss.

Chapter Two

JENNA HADN'T BEEN KIDDING when she'd told Meemee to write down she was a white picket fence kind of woman, Sully thought as early the next morning he gazed at the newly painted white picket fence enveloping the cozy century home on the corner of Lilac Lane and Peppermint Trail. A colorful sign, splashed with the words *Jenna's Antiques and Collectibles* hung over the fancy, white screen door.

The house looked vanilla yet sexy at the same time.

He'd passed by the place many times since he'd been back, but he'd never gone inside. Not until the time had been right, and today...it was right.

He'd known she'd dated several local guys while he'd been away. Letters from Meemee had kept him up to speed about Jenna MacLean, whether he'd wanted to hear about her or not.

When his contract with NASA had been up for renewal, he'd opted out and come straight back to Hideaway.

Back to Jenna.

But try as he might, he hadn't been able to seek her out and apologize for breaking up with her the way he had, for leaving her and for crushing the promises he'd made to her.

Apologies had always been hard for him. Stubborn Hero pride, his mother always called it. She'd warned him many times his pride would get him into trouble.

Looks like she'd been right.

Sully's heart picked up a mad pace as he caught sight of the two white-painted, fan-back settees on the front porch and the twig heart busting with ivy hanging on the wall between the chairs. It looked like a nice place for a couple to sit during romantic evenings. His cock hardened at the thought of Jenna and himself sitting there, talking of what they would do with each other when they hit the sheets for the night.

He shook his head in frustration. He had no business chasing after Jenna MacLean. He didn't need her, didn't need the complication of love in his life again. Nor did he need the pain of a broken heart should she choose not to give them a second chance and that was only if he ever gathered up the nerve to ask her to take him back.

And then there was the Ménage Club. The possibilities of pleasuring Jenna using the club were endless.

Although she'd mentioned in her ad she would participate in ménages, if they got together and she discovered he wanted help from a third in their relationship from the Club, would she tell him to go to hell?

Or would she submit?

They'd been apart for so long. It was obvious from that napkin she'd changed, matured. Did she even want him back in her life? Was it not crazy of him to think they could simply pick up where they'd left off? To give their relationship another try based on a club that used extreme techniques to bring a couple back together?

He should just keep on walking. Pass the cute, little antiques shop and the life she'd built without him, and never look back.

Sully frowned as delicate perfume wafted up from the carefully tended flowerbeds. Once upon a time, he'd dreamed of a place like this. Dreamed of a woman like Jenna.

Old-fashioned yet sexually adventurous.

And then he'd met Jenna and his dreams had come half true, but because of her jealousy and his inability to reassure her she was number one in his life, he'd turned his back on her. He'd joined NASA's new astronaut training program that had promised great pay, big space adventures, astronaut training and a way to forget about Jenna.

Yeah, he'd gotten the great pay, space adventure and training, but his heart and bed had been empty without her. Maybe it was better for her if he just stayed away. Maybe it was best if he just kept on walking and walked right out of her life.

THE SOUND OF THE BELL jangling against the front door to the store made Jenna lift her head from the items she'd been unpacking in the back room.

"I'll be there in a minute!" she called out and returned her gaze to the yellowware dish set. The set was fantastic and in prime condition. She already had a buyer for it. She would get a great profit since she'd gotten it for peanuts. Not to mention the other goodies she'd purchased. A 1740s pewter cupboard, the Connecticut saltbox that was used as a hideout for the Tories during the Revolution then used to hide the Civil War slaves, and many other items that would sell like hotcakes this summer when the tourists came to the quaint little town of Hideaway, Maine.

Taking a quick sip of her strawberry cooler, she then made her way to the main room.

Hmm...no one here. They must have gone into one of the other areas in her shop. She'd arranged the entire first floor of the old century house using a theme for each room. The living room was the first room the customers saw when they came in. She'd crammed it with antique wingback chairs, a gorgeous sofa, a fish-packing crate she'd found at an out-of-town antiques fair. Among other things, she had a variety of antique kerosene lamps strewn about for effect, spinning wheels, late nineteenth-century cast-iron urns, a weaver's frame with hand-carved spools for the wool and tons of vintage bottles that cast jewellike hues as they sat on glass shelves in the numerous windows.

As she zipped through the kitchen, she glanced at the decorative old copper pots and pans hanging from a hook lamp, the bright antique pottery displays sitting on the kitchen countertops or her prized possession—a cast-iron beauty of an aged stove made in the early 1900s.

She peeked into the various other rooms before spotting someone in the back bedroom. Ah, so this is where her customer had gotten off to. He stood with his broad back to her and even before she recognized his dark brown, short hair and the confident way he stood as he surveyed the 1890s canopy bed she'd decorated with a late nineteenth-century, finely stitched tulip quilt, her pulse was already racing.

"It must have taken a lot of work to put this place together," Sully said.

He didn't turn around when he spoke. Instead, he reached out a large hand and ran his fingers tenderly over the quilt.

Jenna swallowed at the sensual gesture.

Suddenly she for his fingers to touch her heated skin, cup her breasts, rub her clit.

Oh boy! Not good.

"May I help you?" she whispered in a sultry voice. She forced herself to quickly clear her throat, to push aside the wicked sensations running through her as she stood in a bedroom with her sexy Sully.

"Actually, yes. There are a few interesting items here I could use in my bar...as conversation pieces."

He strolled to a nearby Pennsylvania cupboard where she had housed some of her antique erotic toys. She'd debated long and hard whether or not to invest in such intimate items. To her surprise, they were some of her hottest sellers.

Most people bought them as keepsakes to remind them of the old days or like Sully, who wanted them as conversation pieces.

Now as he touched her sex toys, he was turning her on big-time.

Good grief, just looking at his broad back, the arrogant slash of his bristled jaw, the gentle way his fingers wrapped around the wooden egg-shaped item as he scooped it into his large, calloused palm made her mind scramble into a whirlwind of thoughts.

What if he decided to throw her on to the bed and have his way with her? What if she broke down and asked him to take her back? Told him she really wanted to be with him. To experiment with him at the Ménage Club. A club that was rumored to have a 100% success rate for bringing together old lovers who'd sworn never to get back together again.

"What's this?" he asked as his hot, green gaze slammed into her, making her catch her breath.

Damn him for being so curious.

She should tell him it was a Fabergé egg, just to be rude or to tease him, but he was a potential customer and she needed to keep herself in business mode.

Sully Hero was a well-liked man in this town and if he could spread word about her antiques shop, it could only be beneficial to be nice and pretend her insides weren't shaking with both lust and fear that he would recognize she wanted to reignite the passion they'd once shared. But she couldn't afford to have him break her heart when he took off again. Maybe next time he'd be gone for good.

"It's a Victorian-era butt plug," she admitted.

"Really?" One side of his luscious mouth quirked upward and her heart went into hyper mode. He'd always looked so damn cute when he threw her that teasing smile. It just about made her knees melt.

"Yes. A European doctor invented this particular shape. He prescribed them to couples as a kind of fertility aid to help prevent sperm loss. The idea of the inserted egg into a woman's anus would make her vagina tighter and this butt plug would make the sperm head toward the woman's reproductive organs."

He merely nodded, acting as if speaking about butt plugs were a perfectly normal event for him.

She, however, could feel her face heating up. Whether from excitement or embarrassment, she wasn't too sure. And sweet heavens she couldn't believe she was speaking so casually about sex toys with him. In the past, it had been a topic of conversation she'd avoided like the plague...until she'd read on the Internet that sex toys were a perfectly natural addition to millions of couples' sex lives and it wasn't something shameful or scandalous as her late grandmother had made her believe when she'd discovered the tiny vibrator in Jenna's room—the vibrator Sully had bought her.

"And what's this?" He picked up a long, thick, ivory item.

Oh, God!

"A...a Renaissance Italian dildo." Have mercy, now it really was getting hot in here!

"Tell me more about it."

Keep it businesslike, Jen. If he buys one, you'll be making a tidy profit.

"Well...back then they were called *diletto*, which means delight. Skilled craftsmen made them out of stone, leather, ivory and wood. Olive oil was used as a lubricant."

Her pussy spasmed at the thought of Sully inserting the dildo into her eager and craving vagina.

"And this?"

Oh my! Her throat suddenly grew dry as he set down the dildo and picked up an ivory ring.

"It's from the 1600s."

"Exquisite carving...looks like a dragon."

"It is." To her horror her voice cracked. She cleared her tight throat and forced herself to remain calm. Heck, she wasn't doing a good job of it, at least not by the look of her reflection in a nearby mirror.

Oh, God! Her cheeks were pink and her swollen breasts were heaving wildly against her suddenly too tight granny dress. Not to mention her pussy was creaming up a hot storm.

"What was it used for?"

Use your imagination! she wanted to yell. Instead, she found herself explaining, totally mesmerized at the lusty interest sparkling his eyes.

"Men would slip it over their...erections in order to hold them longer."

Sully moved closer to her, his gaze narrowing as he looked more closely at the object.

"An antique cock ring. And what about this nub here? It looks like a clitoris stimulator."

Her pussy creamed harder as she imagined slipping the cock ring onto Sully's penis. Imagined his huge cock sliding in and out of her quivering vagina for hours as the cock ring maintained his erection, the nub on the end of it massaging her into one mind-blowing orgasm after another.

She noticed how good he smelled. His masculine scent teased her senses, made her want to inhale deep and hard, made her want to melt against him and feel him rub that big bulge in his pants against her pussy.

"Jenna?" His sexy voice shattered her fantasy.

She blinked and looked into his eyes. They were dark with sexual intent.

Hunger and raw, fierce need grabbed her. Instantly she was lost in sensations. Lost in lust. Lost in love.

Good grief! Was she nuts? Sully was no good for her! She'd taken years to get over him...hell, who was she kidding? She'd never gotten over him. Their years apart had only made her crave him more, had made her study sex toys and their history just so she would be ready for a moment like this. Now that the time had come, she wasn't prepared for the sparks of attraction bursting between them. Nor was she prepared to lose herself inside these wonderful sensations.

Her nostrils flared at his primitive, male scent. Her breasts felt all tingly as his gaze drifted to them. She managed to take a step backward and felt the bureau press erotically against her ass. Her face grew warmer as he watched her closely. Too closely.

"Yes, the nub would rub against the woman's clit," she admitted.

It would rub against her clit. One brilliant orgasm after another while Sully watched.

"Enhancing her pleasure, no doubt."

"No doubt," she agreed.

He grinned. The intimate smile sunk deep into her very core, making her body hum. He placed the item back on the shelf, only to pick up yet another toy.

"What would this be used for?" he asked as he lifted the rubber penis-shaped item and examined it. "It's hollow. Wide opening. Wide enough to slip over a man's cock. Is it a cock massager of some sort?"

Sweet heavens! She couldn't hold out too much longer against him.

"Actually no, it's The Penis Stiffener, patented in 1907 in the United States."

"Exactly what's that?"

"It was used by men with...erection problems." Of which, Sully still had no problem in that area, if the huge, quickly growing bulge between his legs was any indication.

"And the smaller opening at the other end?"

"To allow the sperm through and into a woman's vagina."

"Very nice invention. Which leads me to my next question."

"Wh-What's that?"

He'd placed The Penis Stiffener onto the bureau and maneuvered himself in front of her. His body heat slammed into her like a seductive lover as both his arms came around to her sides, his hands settling on the bureau, effectively holding her hostage.

Oh boy.

"Why the interest in antique sex toys, Jenna? Why the ad on the napkin last night?"

Your sexual tastes have changed, Jenna. Big-time! Are you dating anyone special? Will you let me fuck you right now, right here? Or will you turn me away? He hadn't said anything, but she could literally hear his unspoken words and questions sizzle through the air between them.

"Actually, it really is none of your business."

His scorching gaze once again traveled to where her breasts were pushing violently against her granny dress as she tried desperately to inhale fresh air. But his strong, masculine scent was everywhere, calling to her, telling her to move closer to him.

"Actually, I think it is my business," he whispered.

His large hands suddenly lifted and she exhaled a slow, aroused breath as he ran his fingers through her hair, holding her head hostage.

Her heart thumped as his lips parted. "As a customer, I have every right to know where you get your information from and why your interests lie in antique sex toys."

He leaned closer. Her pulse skipped erratically and she received an awesome view of the gold flecks in the dark green of his eyes. His erotic scent swarmed her. Encouraged her to part her lips in answer.

He was a bastard to do this to her. But what a hunky bastard.

He came down.

His lips were warm. Oh, so damned warm. His mouth smoothed over hers in such an intimate caress her knees weakened.

In a split second she was torn. Torn by her need to be with him again. Torn by her fear of being hurt again. Her need won out.

Wrapping her arms around his neck, partly to keep herself from dropping to the ground as her knees continued to melt, but mostly because she didn't want him to pull away.

She loved the silky feel of his short hair brushing against her hands. Enjoyed the way her fingers tingled as she touched the bare flesh of his sinewy neck, the hot, male muscles of his strong shoulders.

His mouth savored her. His carnal-shaped lips sliding, tasting, exploring, sending raw desire coursing through her mouth. Her breasts. Her pussy.

Damn! He made her feel so aware of her sexuality as his tasty mouth held hers captive. She was enjoying this so much it made her heady. Made her want to hop up onto the bureau. Made her want to spread her legs and allow him to come inside her.

"I've missed kissing you, Jenna," Sully whispered as he licked her tingling lips with his moist tongue.

Before she could tell him she missed him too, his mouth latched onto hers again. His strong, delicious tongue pushed past her lips and slid against her teeth. His breath was so hot against her face. The yearning to have his cock buried deep inside her grew even stronger.

She should be pushing him away, pounding her fists against his solid chest, demanding to know why he'd come back to town when he'd told her he would never return.

Instead, she melted against his hard length. Responding. Returning a tentative kiss. As she kissed him back, he groaned a virile sound of unleashed passion. Jenna's pussy pulsed at the erotic sound.

His hands slid from her tangled hair and his long, tender fingers trailed down the side of her neck. A moment later, she could feel his fingers fumbling with the granny buttons on the front of her dress. She wanted to help him, but his intoxicating kisses kept her from moving, kept her trapped and at his mercy.

Mild air pressed against her bare shoulders and she realized he was trying to push the garment down her shoulders. Reluctantly she let go of his neck and dropped her arms, splaying her hands onto his narrow waist, allowing him easy access.

Her breath stilled as his big fingers worked the front clasp on her lacy bra. When her breasts fell free, hot hands cupped them. The sensual touch fried her blood. The heat of him made her cry out. He quickly drowned her sob as his mouth captured hers once again.

Instantly any resolve she may have had about not letting him near her vanished as his masculine burn zipped through her flesh.

"You're tense, Jenna. Too tense. Are you afraid of me?" His softly whispered words against her mouth made her shake her head in response.

"Do you mind me touching your breasts?"

Again she shook her head, staring into his startling green eyes, wondering why he was being such a darned gentleman when, instead, she wished for him to be fierce with her as he'd been in the past, craving him to caress her breasts and take her roughly the way he'd always done.

He pressed the top of his forehead against hers, a past indication that she should look down. Watch what he did to her breasts. The gesture was all too familiar and suddenly it felt as if they'd never been apart.

Oh, God, she should be pulling away. Telling him exactly where he should go. Instead, she looked down as she'd always done in the past. Looked down and watched the erotic sight that had always sent hot, jumbled need shooting through her.

Her body shook with remembrance as his palms held her breasts captive. His fingers and thumbs tweaked her aching nipples, drew them out until they were rosy red. Until exquisite pleasure-pain erupted. Until that invisible line of erotic longing burn straight down her lower belly and deep into her clenching pussy.

The son of a bitch always knew just what buttons to push to turn her on or, in her case, what nipples to squeeze to make her hot and hungry. To make all coherent thoughts fly to the wind.

Oh, yes! This felt so heavenly! Much better than her nipple clamps.

His long fingers massaged her mounds, traced her areolas until Jenna swore her breasts felt twice their normal size and her nipples were peaked, aching to be touched some more.

He licked her lips, her cheeks, her neck, moving due south. Long, erotic strokes, his moist tongue dabbing at her flesh like little blades of fire. Wet fire that also erupted inside her pussy.

When his tongue swiped across one of her nipples, her bud tingled from the warmth. The need to have his mouth feast upon every inch of her flesh was so great she could literally feel the raw tingling sensations of need slide through her, take her over.

His luscious mouth quickly latched onto a lollipop-sized nipple.

"Oh, sweet mercy!" she couldn't help but cry out as intense heat zapped through her nipple sending her senses into hyperawareness. She bucked against his face. Instinctively she rubbed her breast against the roughness of his five o'clock shadow until her flesh burned and ached.

Until she breathed rapidly. Until lust ravished her senses.

God! He'd always made her feel so incredibly horny. Always made her lose control.

The sucking sounds of his mouth feasting upon her breast intermingled with the faraway sound of jangling bells. The sound barely registered upon her senses. At least not until she felt Sully's lips stiffen against her aroused breast. She cried out in distress as his succulent mouth let her nipple go with a pop, and it slowly registered through her erotic haze exactly what the jangling sound entailed.

A customer.

Oh, my God!

She'd become so lost in her arousal she'd forgotten anyone could come into the antiques shop.

She pushed Sully away, trying hard to ignore his amused grin.

Anxiety gripped her as her gaze flew to the bedroom door, fully expecting someone to walk in on them. God! Wouldn't her customer be shocked to find her there with her breasts hanging out of her dress, her nipples red and swollen from Sully's suckling?

"I'll take all of the items we talked about." Although he sounded all business, as if nothing had just happened, she could hear his harsh breathing, could see the blush of redness in his lips, the swelling from their kisses. Her mouth probably looked the same.

And, good heavens, she could see the intense erection pressing against his jeans. Her customer would know what they'd been doing!

Get a grip, girl! Your grandmother's stern principles are rearing their ugly head again. Who cares about what the customer thinks!

"Are you sure?" she said, her face heating as with trembling fingers she hooked up her bra and buttoned her dress, avoiding his searing gaze.

"Very." He grabbed the cock ring and the other items he wanted to purchase and cradled them in his arms. He acted as if he belonged there, as if it were perfectly normal for him to come into her shop, feast upon her breasts and stand there with an armload of antique sex toys.

Confusion slammed into her.

For goodness' sake! She'd just let Sully Hero seduce her breasts with his mouth! Why? Why had she allowed him to do what he wanted to do so damned easily? She should have protested. Should have pushed him away or, at the very least, slapped his face for making her succumb to these fantastic desires once again.

"We'd better hurry. You have a customer," he prodded.

Shit! Her customer!

She had better get her ass in gear and quit lounging around in the bedroom, craving more of these unwanted attentions from him.

She had to act like a professional. This was a small town after all. If a client even suspected she and Sully were doing something inappropriate in one of her antique-laden bedrooms, it would be all over town within minutes.

She forced herself to snap into business mode. "If you'd like to follow me, I'll ring up your purchases."

"Sure thing."

Jenna could literally feel his scorching gaze caress her ass as she walked down the hallway. A wonderful splash of excitement gripped her at the thought of him finding out she wasn't as prim and proper as she'd once been. The thong she wore beneath her granny dress and the belly button ring she'd given to herself as a birthday present last year would attest to that fact. Stronger waves of desire swept through her at the thought of him pressing the egg-shaped Victorian-era butt plug into her virgin ass, as per the European doctor's instruction. And then her Hero sliding his big, rigid cock into her vagina.

Pressing, pushing, pumping. Frantically thrusting his hips as he led both of them toward an exquisite orgasm.

Suddenly Jenna craved that frozen bottle of beer she'd been wanting last night in Sully's bar when he'd read her ad on the napkin.

"Hello, Jenna, Sullivan," came elderly Mrs. Hero's soft voice as they erupted into the living room where she kept the cash register just beside the front entrance of her antiques shop. She noticed Sully's grandmother's eyes widen with surprise and his grandfather's knowing smile when they spotted their grandson following her, his arms laden with antique sex toys.

Jenna's face grew even hotter.

Shit! Was this embarrassing or what? Sully's own grandparents witnessing what he was purchasing. He, however, didn't seem the least bit fazed by their appearance as he grinned happily and dropped the toys onto the counter. He quickly gave his petite gray-haired grandmother a big bear hug and slapped his tall grandfather on his shoulder with affection as they greeted each other warmly.

As quickly as she could, Jenna grabbed the erotic toys and settled them on a chair behind the counter, out of sight. The last thing she wanted to do was mortify the couple, especially since they came from the same generation as her grandmother, where sex hadn't been as free as it was today.

"Please, there's no need to be embarrassed, dear," Mrs. Hero said. Jenna's face burned as three sets of Hero eyes looked at her. "We've been married for more years than either of your ages. Nothing surprises us, especially the fact that our grandson is purchasing such interesting items."

She turned to look up at Sully, who towered over the petite woman. "Shouldn't you be purchasing modern sex toys instead of antique ones?"

His grandfather chuckled as Sully frowned. Was that a blush teasing his cheeks?

Jenna bit her lip to prevent herself from laughing out loud. Confident, sexy Sully Hero could actually blush.

"I take it you've been keeping Jenna busy with those toys?" Mr. Hero, an elderly version of Sully's sexy looks asked.

Oh, God! These folks sure did have an interesting sense of humor. They didn't seem the least put off at Sully's interest in sex toys.

"We've been having an interesting time of it. We were getting...reacquainted."

"How exciting!" Both Mr. and Mrs. Hero grinned with approval.

Oh, no! She needed to change the subject and fast. The last thing she wanted was for them to get their hopes up. They'd always treated her so kindly, had expected she and Sully would eventually get married. They'd been devastated at the news of their breakup.

"I'm glad you came in," Jenna said quickly. "I was going to call you, Mrs. Hero. About the yellowware set you were enquiring about a few weeks ago."

"You found a set?" Her eyes twinkled with happiness.

"It's in the back, if you'd like to take a look at it. I can bring it out as soon as I ring through Sully."

The elderly lady clasped her hands together with obvious delight. "Oh, I'm so excited."

"If I'd known you'd get excited over a yellowware dish set, I would have bought you one," Mr. Hero chuckled, amusement flashed in his eyes.

"You already bought me one shortly after we were married, don't you remember?" Mrs. Hero frowned with obvious disappointment.

"Oh, yeah, whatever happened to it?"

"I threw the dishes at you that night you came home drunk without a paycheck."

"I can't seem to remember that." He threw Jenna and Sully a quick wink.

"Don't be fooled by him. He remembers and he never did that again. It was during the Depression. He'd been laid-off for months and just called back to work. It was his first paycheck and he'd gotten drunk and gambled it away."

"Actually, I gambled it away then got drunk on the last dollar."

Mrs. Hero grinned at his admission and, to Jenna's surprise, she wrapped her arms around the tall man and gave him an affectionate hug.

"When he came home and explained what happened, I threw every piece of the yellowware set at him. Broke everything. The way I saw it, if there was no money for food, why bother to have any dishes?"

"I learned how to move really fast that night," he said, returning her hug. The elderly couple gazed into each other's eyes, seemingly oblivious of Jenna and Sully watching them. Or at least Jenna had been watching them. When she looked up, she discovered Sully's hot gaze traveling down the length of her body then drew back to connect with hers, sending a lightning storm of heat zipping through her.

Irritation nibbled at her nerves. She shouldn't be reacting this way every time he looked at her. She should be immune to his hungry gaze, to his hot, wild kiss, to the erotic way his sensual mouth had just latched onto her nipples only moments earlier in the bedroom.

"They never go to bed mad at each other," Sully explained. She detected anger beneath his controlled voice. Anger directed at her, no doubt. They'd had many fights when they'd gone out together. She didn't like the fact he had women friends and he didn't like the fact she was sexually uptight. He'd wanted more than she'd been willing to give at the time. They'd both been too proud to apologize after their fights, until the need for the fantastic sex they always experienced together had arisen, then they'd always managed to run into each other again and make up.

Unfortunately having great sex didn't a relationship make...at least it hadn't worked for them in the past and she doubted things had changed very much between them, especially at the fact of her red-hot anger popping its nasty little head up at seeing him talking with that blonde beauty last evening at his bar.

"On our wedding night we vowed to never go to bed mad at each other, no matter how big the fight," Mrs. Hero explained.

"We were both too stubborn to break that promise," her husband chuckled. They were still locked in an affectionate embrace.

"That's the secret to our long marriage," she smiled.

"It's a lovely tradition." Jenna grinned, feeling the warmth of their happiness sift through her. However, her warmth disintegrated at Sully's cool voice.

"Too bad more couples don't adopt that tradition."

His searing gaze once again traveled over the length of her, leaving her both breathless at the intensity of his scorching look and also insulted at his words. Not to mention she was getting the distinct feeling he thought their final breakup was all her fault.

"I've got several errands to run. Can I pick the stuff up afterwards?" *So we can pick up where we left off?* He didn't need to say it, she could read the lusty message flashing in his eyes. But she was pissed off at his comment about adopting a tradition of not going to bed angry at each other. The dissolution of their relationship hadn't been all her fault. Besides, she was not in the mood for "making up" and starting the same pattern as they'd done in the past.

Fighting. Having great sex. Fighting. Having great sex.

"You can pay upon delivery. I'll drop it by the bar tonight," Jenna told him tightly, suddenly eager to get rid of Sully before her temper exploded and they started rehashing old times in front of his grandparents.

"Okay, I'll see you at the bar, tonight." Sully turned to his grandparents and smiled warmly to the elderly couple. "I'll see both of you later."

His grandparents didn't seem the least bit put off at the tension zipping between Jenna and Sully as he bid them goodbye.

The minute the bell jangled his exit Jenna knew exactly what question was coming.

"Are the two of you back together?" Mrs. Hero asked, hopefulness washing across both their faces. Guilt slammed into her and she almost lied. Almost told them that Sully and she were on friendly terms again, but Sully's little snap a moment earlier had just bought all the hurt and frustration to the surface. Hurt because it seemed he thought everything had been her fault and frustration because she thought that too. It had taken her four years to realize when a relationship broke up it wasn't just one person's fault.

It takes two to tango. Her best friend Meemee had told her that over and over again every time Jenna broke it off with a local guy—especially after things started to get a little too serious for her comfort.

She forced herself back to the present. Back to reality.

"No, we aren't back together and don't expect us to, either."

Both of them looked devastated. Oh, God, now she felt really bad.

"But at least we're on speaking terms, that's a good sign."

"You're more than halfway there," Mrs. Hero burst out.

I wish you were right, Jenna thought to herself, suddenly wishing she and Sully were together again, but that could never happen, not unless they got a miracle. Sully was obviously still carrying around anger toward her because of the way things ended between them, and she seemed to always sense it in him and became angry herself. It was a no-win situation.

"I'll go get you that yellowware set so you can take a look at it. Back in a minute."

Besides, she thought as she hurried toward the back room, she never wanted to experience the searing hurt she'd gone through after their last and final breakup. As far as she was concerned, that fact alone should be enough of a reason never to let Sully Hero back into her heart...or her bed.

Chapter Three

"SO? DID YOU GO AND see Jenna?" Tony asked as Sully threw himself into the secluded booth of his bar so they could talk.

"And did you find the napkin with her ad?" Meemee asked as she made a mad grab for the frosty beer he'd just brought her.

"Yes, on both counts," he admitted.

"And?" both of them asked at the same time.

Sully couldn't help but laugh at the excitement these two shared in helping to get Jenna and himself back together. For good this time.

"Easy, guys. One at a time."

"Me first," Meemee said quickly. "Did you get the napkin I left?"

"You left it?"

"Jeez, don't sound so disappointed." Meemee threw him her famous pout. Her full, red lips going into a downward spiral. The sight of her doing that consistently seemed to cheer him up. She was always such an outgoing person and even when she tried to pout, the happiness in her just seemed to shine through, giving her an even cuter appearance. He was sure guys she dated loved to tease her just to see that sexy pout.

"No, it's not that... I..." He had hoped Jenna might have left it for him to find. "Yes, I got it."

"Good, then you know what's she's looking for. Now all you have to do is supply it."

She made it sound so damn easy. She was such a romantic. She'd been an avid fan of Jenna and him getting back together. She'd almost given him a heart attack with her excitement when he'd called her, told her he was coming back for Jenna and wanted the help of the Ménage Club that Tony not only created but also ran out of his beach house.

He'd hurt Jenna terribly by running off the way he had. She was an extremely sensitive woman, especially about her weight and ultra-sensitive in the way he kidded around with his women friends. It wouldn't be easy to regain Jenna's trust. But he knew in his heart he wanted her, loved her, and this time around, he was willing to go to extremes to get her and to keep her.

"So? How did your meeting with her go this morning? Did you start phase one of the body seduction?" Tony asked. Sully ignored the way Meemee leaned closer, her eyes wide with expectation. She was also a member of the Club, helping couples through their troubled relationships, but she'd kept her membership a secret from Jenna and him until she'd finally mentioned she was a member in the last letter she'd sent to him.

"Normally, I'm not a guy who kisses and tells," he said truthfully. "But since the Club's motto is to be honest at all costs... I had her in the palms of my hands...literally."

Tony grinned. "You work fast, my young apprentice."

"I fucked up."

"How?" Meemee asked.

"When I left her, we were both pissed off. Just like old times. It's like we can pick up on each other's moods or something, and then we both act on it."

Tony nodded. "You two are both on the same level. So in tune with each other. It may not seem like it now, but in the future, as you learn to trust one another, this gift will cement your relationship."

"Did you speak to her about the Ménage Club?" Meemee asked.

"No, like I said, I got sidetracked and then we got interrupted."

"Well, she is a beautiful, curvy woman," Tony said. "I can see why it would be hard to keep your hands off her, but you must remain focused on our goal. You must remember what you've been taught by us. The whole theory behind the Ménage Club is to discover both of your underlying fears and bring them to the surface. To treat these fears in a world of pleasure and affection. That will make each of you vulnerable and open to the other. Then and only then will you both be able to change and ultimately trust each other. In short, capture her body first, her heart will quickly follow and, eventually, you will win her trust."

"All this ménage stuff is just too unbelievable to work, it just seems all backward. I mean you're supposed to fall in love first and then have sex, and then maybe a ménage if both parties agree but this..." He shrugged and cursed silently at all the insecurities starting to flood him.

"That's the old-fashioned side of you talking. You want Jenna, don't you?" Meemee grinned, knowing what his answer would be.

Frustration grabbed at his gut making him wince. "With every breath of my being. But—"

"No 'buts', Sully," Tony broke in. "As you've told us, your old-fashioned ways haven't worked for you—it's time to try our techniques. Remember we've been one hundred percent successful and we sure as hell aren't going to let you two be the first to break our record."

"If the Ménage Club is so successful, then why aren't the two of you hitched?"

A dark frown of pain flashed between the two of them leaving Sully wishing he hadn't asked. Both of them had lost the loves of their lives. Meemee's fiancé had run off with Tony's fiancée while Tony had been away on his last space assignment.

"That's why we're there, Sully," Tony replied. "Why I gave up NASA and created the Club. To help others get back together. We've all lost someone we love in one way or the other, with the barest of chances to get them back. While we train with couples, we learn about relationships ourselves. When we think we are ready, we pursue the partner we wouldn't have had a chance with otherwise."

"Enough about us," Meemee broke in. "We need to figure out another way for you two to meet."

"She's making a delivery to the bar tonight with some stuff I bought at her store."

"Good. Are you ready for her?" he asked.

Sully nodded and fought against the excitement that was quickly building at the thought of his next meeting with Jenna.

He grinned at his two friends. "She won't know what hit her."

DESPITE HER EARLIER sane ideas of not jumping back into bed with Sully, Jenna's heart picked up a mad speed as she swung her truck into the dark lane that led to the back entrance of Sully's bar. She'd opted to come this way in order to avoid the crush of people who were sure to be there. All she'd have to do is slip in the back door and find Sully, which should be easy enough. Ever since he'd bought the place and reopened last month, the few times she'd come there she'd seen him flirting with some long-legged woman or another at his bar. A fissure of jealousy slithered through her at the thought of finding him amusing himself with yet another woman. He seemed to do it easily enough, had given her a firsthand look as he'd so efficiently kissed her breathless back at her antiques shop. Before she'd known it, he'd unbuttoned her dress and had had his way with her breasts.

She moaned out loud as she remembered the seductive way his lips had clamped and captured each of her buds, teasing them with his raspy tongue, tormenting her until she was a torrid bundle of need.

Bastard! He was good. So damn good. He'd always known her weakness for sex even when she'd denied it to herself. Truth be known, she craved to be pleasured by Sully.

But not tonight. Tonight she'd be as solid as a stone toward him.

Yeah, right. That's why she'd changed into a sexy black dress that flattered her generous breasts and made her big butt look just a tad thinner. Not to mention her pussy was trembling with anticipation as she hungered to see his eyes flash with lust the instant he saw her.

Cursing herself for being so damned weak, she parked her truck, hoisted the small box containing his toys into the crook of one arm and got out of her vehicle. Except for the screen door, the back entrance was open. She'd expected to hear rowdy music drifting out, but she heard nothing as she opened the door and let herself inside.

There was also an absence of people talking and she wondered what the hell was going on. The hallway looked ultra-clean and smelled really nice too as she walked farther into the establishment.

"Hello! Delivery from Jenna's Antiques and Collectibles," she called out, her voice echoing through the silent hallway.

"Back here, in the kitchen!" came his shout. "Just set it on the bar, I'll be out in a minute."

Gosh, he even yelled good. His smooth, rich voice just made her skin tingle wonderfully all over.

She entered the bar area and frowned.

Empty. The dammed place was empty! That meant they would be alone.

Oh dear.

Insecurities pushed away the confidence she'd had building throughout the day. Maybe she should get out of there? Maybe she really wasn't prepared to be alone with him again?

"Gone out of business already?" she teased and settled the box on to the counter. "I'll just leave it on the bar. You can catch me with the money another time."

The faster she got out of there, the safer her heart would be.

Before she could spin around and leave, he appeared in a nearby doorway, totally shirtless.

Oh, double dear.

His gorgeous shoulder muscles rippled as he dried his hands on a towel and her attention immediately drew to his chest, to the soft dusting of curly hair and the smooth bunch of muscles swelling there.

"My cook just quit on me and the water main broke. No water. Had to close the bar."

"Oh."

Talk about a wonderfully sculpted chest. Was that soft-looking, downy chest hair still as soft and silky as she remembered?

"Thanks for bringing the toys, Jenna."

He smiled as he walked toward her. The smile didn't reach his eyes. Instead, raw, burning lust burned there. Lust and affection and appreciation.

"You look really hot in black, Jenna."

She did? She pushed aside her self-doubts. Of course she did! That's why she'd picked this dress.

"Thank you for noticing," she whispered, eagerly and stupidly accepting his compliment.

Whew! He looked hot in the way he moved. Sexy. Sensual. A man on a mission of seduction perhaps?

Her pulse fluttered.

He popped open the box containing the erotic toys and he examined each one. His large hands handled the items gently, intimately.

"I put a cabinet in the corner for these toys," he said softly, and pointed to the secluded corner near the jukebox.

Anyone using the music machine would certainly get an eyeful when they passed the glass-enclosed cabinet.

"Want to help me arrange them? I could use a woman's touch."

She bet he could.

He was topless, wearing a scorching gaze—not to mention they were totally alone—and he was asking her to stay.

God, she wanted to stay. To see where things would lead. To have some red-hot maintenance sex with him and then simply walk away, but she could see herself falling head over heels for him again.

"Jenna? Are you okay? It looks like you zoned out on me for a second."

"I'm fine, just fine." She plastered on a fake smile, although she could feel a hand squeezing her heart for what could have been between them.

"You sure?"

Damn him. He'd always been so in tune to her feelings.

"I should leave."

"Meaning you don't really want to."

Bold son of a bitch, wasn't he?

"C'mon, let's set the toys up."

To her surprise, his fingers intertwined with hers.

Hot was her first thought as his grip tightened around her hand. He picked up the box she'd just delivered and pulled her toward the cabinet. *Desperate* was her second thought as she noticed the delicious bulge pressed boldly against the prison restraint of his pants.

Whew! Warm in here, isn't it?

He let her go and tilted the box on the jukebox. Cupping the Victorian-era butt plug, he lifted it out of the tissue paper.

"Top, middle or bottom shelf?"

"Middle shelf. Most people probably wouldn't know what it is, so it's best to put something more recognizable at eye level on the top shelf."

"Oh, yes, I forgot to tell you. They'll know what these antique items are and where I got them." He reached into his back pocket and produced some of her fancy little business cards. She hadn't noticed he'd picked some up. There were some index cards too.

"You remembered everything I told you," she laughed as she read each of the cards stating the information she'd told him about the European doctor's butt plug and the other items he'd purchased.

He grinned as he positioned the items on the shelf where she suggested and she placed the appropriate card with the item.

"I'll have to come over for more sex toys," he said softly after he was finished. Now why did she get the feeling he wasn't talking about her antique sex toys but her personal toys?

She inhaled sharply at that thought and smelled his masculine scent.

Strong. Powerful. Sensual. Her body clenched erotically, heat gripped her veins, preparing her.

"Maybe you've got some anal beads or a vibrator lying around in that store of yours?"

He'd come closer. When had he come so close? They were practically touching each other.

Lusty sensations swept around her. Her breathing quickened. His eyes darkened with need. Dilated with desire.

Oh, sweet heavens, help her. She didn't want to be swept away with this need of being in his arms again, didn't want her nipples tightening with the delicious craving of having his hot, succulent mouth on her breasts again, his thick, hard cock penetrating her, her self-control vanishing...

She swallowed against the ache of touching him, tried to dampen the desire swirling around her.

It didn't work.

She dropped her truck keys. Barely heard them clatter to the floor as his mouth came down hard on hers. Harder than the gentle kiss he'd given her in her shop earlier that day. The erotic sensations threw her off balance and instinctively she melted against him.

Gosh! This was the Sully she remembered.

Demanding. Seductive. Fierce with his need to pleasure her—to take pleasure from her.

His lips claimed hers, kissed hers until any focus she might have had disintegrated. Until fire raged through her. Until her knees wobbled and her legs gave out.

On her cry, he caught her. Caught her in his strong, naked arms and carried her to the bar where he hoisted her onto the counter.

She reached out and curled her fingers over the strong, sinewy muscles in his shoulders, spread her legs quickly as his hands touched her knees and he pushed her dress up around her waist.

His hot gaze immediately zeroed in on her belly ring and the tiny gold chain she'd strung through it and wore around her waist. The chain always made her feel feminine and pretty. Always gave her that little satisfaction she knew something that no one else knew about her.

Until now.

Her body hummed at the sight of dark lust splashing in his eyes. His Adam's apple bobbed as he swallowed. She held her breath as he slipped his little finger through the ring and pulled gently, forcing her to move even closer to him.

Masculine heat splashed all around her, his sexy scent made her so hot for him she had to blow out a breath.

"I love this new, daring side to you, Jenna."

"I do too," she admitted.

His finger let go of the ring and he traced a scorching line down her abdomen to touch her thong.

"I've wanted to do this for so damn long," he whispered as his fingers clenched the material and he quickly removed the garment from her, baring her pussy to him.

He swore softly as he noticed she was nude down there. She'd taken to shaving only recently. Perhaps because deep down in her soul she'd held hopes that this day would someday come. Now it was here and her heart hammered violently in her ears and frantically pounded against her chest.

His hands softly stroked her inner thighs, moved inward to her pussy. Sharp sensations ripped through her and she trembled at the intense arousal his tender touches created. Her mouth dropped open in a silent gasp as a finger slid over her sensitive clit.

Immediately she creamed.

He grinned.

Bastard!

He continued.

Slowly sliding. Making her cream harder.

Watching. Pinching softly. Watching.

She burned. Oh, God, did she burn.

Her breath went ragged when his finger slid inside her wet pussy.

She shivered, overwhelmed by his touch. He collected her juices. Used it to massage her ultra-sensitive clit. Lightning strokes of pleasure zipped through her.

Her orgasm was coming already. So quickly.

He shifted and she blinked against the carnal haze enveloping her, moaned as he sat on the barstool, his hot breath exploding against her quivering pussy as his head came down between her spread thighs.

Her lips parted and she could hardly breathe as his tongue slipped inside her vagina.

Touching, stroking, and probing while his finger continued the wicked seduction of her clit.

It felt so good!

She tensed as he worked her. Her eyes closed as the pleasure waves cascaded over her. Her pussy muscles contracted around his tongue. His tongue branded her vagina—his finger tortured her clit.

Instinctively she clamped her legs around his head. The increased pressure was exactly what she needed. She exploded on a cry, loving the pleasure surging through her. Thrusting her pelvis forward into his face, she gyrated her hips mercilessly. She rode his head hard while his lips worshipped her pussy.

He sipped on her labia. Nibbled on her clit and she twisted and whimpered, her hands clenched tightly into fists. Every nerve ending sizzled and she fought to breathe into the pleasure.

When the spasms ebbed, she let her head to loll. Allowed her legs to be pried from around his head.

She sat there on the bar, breathing in and out as she tried desperately to catch her breath.

Man, she felt so weak.

Damn! That felt so good!

She wished she could open her eyes, but she couldn't. They were so heavy lidded. Sully breathed heavily, his breaths caressing her pussy as she kept her legs open to him.

"You always were as weak as a kitten after a climax. It always tamed you, allowed me to do whatever I wanted to you on those occasions when you let me."

She was surprised by the anger etching his voice. "The things I've wanted to do to you, Jenna. Things you wouldn't let me do." *Until now.* He hadn't said it, but the silence that followed said those two words for him.

From somewhere far away, outside her increasing erotic haze, Jenna could hear a phone ringing. Could hear a familiar man's voice echo on the answering machine, a voice she couldn't quite remember.

"Sully? You there? Come on. Pick up the phone, I'm in trouble."

The despair in the man's voice urged Jenna to open her eyes. Sully's gaze was dark and lusty. His lips wet with her cream.

"Ignore him," came Sully's strangled voice as his head descended again.

Oh my gosh! He was going down on her again!

Her pussy quivered with anticipation.

"Sully, answer the damn phone. I need your help. I'm in jail." There was a pregnant pause and that's when she realized who was calling. It was Tony, Sully's best friend. Tony was in love with a woman who wanted nothing to do with him and was now with another man. Sometimes he ended up in jail when he drowned his sorrows in booze and became uncontrollable, even violent.

"Come and bail me out, will you? You gotta come fast. You know how I hate spending the night in jail."

Sully frowned and cursed, his heavy breathing split the silence of the barroom.

"You better answer." Jenna said softly as her bearings slowly returned.

"If he's in jail, I bet there's a woman involved," Sully growled as he slipped off the barstool and headed for the phone.

Probably a redhead. Tony had always preferred redheads. Especially the one he let get away.

"I'm going to have to bail him out, Jenna," Sully growled as he dialed. "Feel free to stay." *So we can pick up where we left off.* Again he didn't say the words, but his carnal look told her everything she needed to know.

"It's better if I go," she said. She needed to be alone, needed to think.

"I'm sorry." He looked it too. There was a disappointed grimace on his face.

She hopped off the bar.

Her legs trembled terribly as she slipped into her thong. Adjusting her clothing, she couldn't stop a wave of anger whispering over her.

He'd already started chatting to the police on the phone and she felt...dismissed. She searched the nearby floor for her keys, found them then headed toward the back door, chastising herself for giving in so easily to her lusty cravings for him. If her grandmother were still alive, she'd be horrified at what she'd let Sully do to her. As it was, she was probably rolling over in her grave.

"I'll walk you to your truck."

He'd come up behind her, his hand braced against the small of her back as he followed her out the back door.

"I want to see you again, Jenna. I'll be in touch."

Before she could so much as mount a protest, his head lowered and his hot mouth seared against hers, capturing her in such a tender kiss that her legs just about gave out. She could taste herself on his lips, a cinnamony-musk mix she found erotic.

He broke the kiss and if he hadn't helped her up into her truck, she surely would have sprawled to the alley pavement.

Sweet Mercy! He knew how to kiss!

"Go home. Get some sleep." *So you're well-rested for what I plan to do to you next time we meet*, his eyes said.

He tapped the hood of her truck and waved. With shaky fingers, she turned on her ignition and watched as he sauntered back into his bar. Heat radiated all around her as she watched him.

Blowing out a tense breath, she pressed her hot forehead against the cool steering wheel. Once again hot moisture was pooling between her legs and her pussy throbbed where his face had just been. Her inner thighs burned, compliments of where his five o'clock shadow had brushed so erotically. She resisted the urge to press her legs together, to bring herself off.

God! She'd just been eaten by Sully Hero!

What had gotten into her? And now she wanted more from him. So much more.

My, oh, my. She was in big trouble.

"JENNA MACLEAN, SPECIAL delivery."

Jenna looked up from the day-old blueberry muffin she'd been staring at while reliving the other night's adventure with Sully to find her best friend Meemee grinning at her from the antiques store back room doorway. She wore her professional, homemade courier uniform; tan slacks and a tan shirt with a colorful nametag proclaiming *Meemee's Courier*.

Gosh! She'd been so deep in thought, wondering why she hadn't heard from Sully in the couple of days since their rendezvous on the bar that she hadn't been aware of the jangle of the bell, signaling someone entering her shop.

"Hey, Meems, what's up?"

"This." She held up a small, slender package of about seven inches long by three inches thick.

Meemee was an entrepreneur in Hideaway. A jill-of-all-trades. Her self-employment jobs included a taxi service, gardening service, as well as the town's only courier service. "The sender requests you open it immediately."

"Who is it from?" Jenna asked when she found no return address on the lightweight item.

"You'll know when you open the package."

Oh, really? How intriguing!

Eagerness to see who was sending her a parcel had her virtually ripping the brown wrapping paper from the box. Who in this town would send her a parcel and instruct her to open it immediately? She did a mental check of the many antiques purchases she'd made. She had plenty on the way but none this small.

Jenna smiled. It had to be from Sully's grandmother. The other day when Jenna had brought out the yellowware set, Mrs. Hero had clasped her hands together and fallen in love with it. Even Mr. Hero had sparkles in his eyes, no doubt remembering the early years of their marriage. They'd purchased the set along with the pretty tulip quilt she'd placed on the canopy bed, the bed in the same bedroom Sully Hero had had his way with her breasts.

God! Just thinking about him made her horny.

She redirected her thoughts back to the parcel. Had Mrs. Hero sent her some of those fresh-baked cornmeal muffins she was so famous for? Her mouth watered at the idea of having a couple of fresh muffins instead of the stale blueberry one she'd brought along for brunch.

Even as she opened the box, she knew it wasn't from Mrs. Hero. It was way too small for muffins. Her mouth dropped open in shock as nestled snugly in blue tissue paper was a slim six-inch long, one-inch wide fuchsia-pink butt plug. On the side, written in bold black letters were the words MÉNAGE CLUB INITIATION.

"Oh, my God," she blurted as shock hit her. It had happened. She'd received an invitation to join Sully at the Ménage Club.

"All right, confess, girlfriend," Meemee said as she too peered inside the box.

"He answered the ad," Jenna replied as her heart slammed up against her chest with such excitement she thought she would pass out.

"What ad?"

"With that cocksure grin plastered all over your face, Meems, I believe you know very well who answered what ad. And you are probably the one who took it out of my purse and gave it back to him."

Meemee shrugged her shoulders and threw Jenna her famous pouty look. "I can't help it if you disappear to go to the bathroom and I happen to need a napkin and look through your purse for one and find the one with your ad and accidentally left it on the table."

"I should have known you were the one who took it!"

Her pout increased.

"What? I did something wrong? Oh! And look the plug comes with instructions."

A cat-got-the-canary grin splashed over Meemee's face as she quickly changed the subject and delicately lifted a paper from the tissue. "This heated, self-lubricating, six-inch butt plug can inflate to eight inches long and to two inches wide," she read. "New superior technology allows the plug to quickly and comfortably inflate and deflate several hundred times a day, allowing a woman's anal muscles to quickly become accustomed to the maximum size within a week."

Meemee blew a stray blonde bang out of her eyes, fanned herself and looked down at Jenna with wide eyes. "Have mercy, best girlfriend, but he is well-hung. I'm so glad he fits at least that part of your ad."

Jenna snatched the paper away from her and read the instructions. Oh, God! Meemee wasn't kidding. There it was in black and white. *Superior technology allows the plug to quickly inflate and deflate...self-lubricating...*

She swallowed at her suddenly dry throat and her ass muscles clenched in wicked anticipation.

"So? Why send you a butt plug? I mean you two split up like years ago. Why is he sending you something so intimate in the mail?"

"It all happened so fast," Jenna confessed.

Meemee's eyebrows furrowed. "What happened so fast?"

"I brought over the erotic toys he'd purchased at the store."

Her eyes widened. "He bought some of your sex toys when he was here? And you just forgot to tell me?"

"It happened so fast."

"God, woman! What happened that he would send you a butt plug instead of roses?"

"Stuff happened. On his bar."

Meemee wiggled her eyebrows in amusement. "*On* his bar? Way to go, Jenna! So? How was it after all this time?"

"Meems, please. What should I do about the plug? Should I send it back?" Even as she asked, she knew she wouldn't send it back. She wanted like crazy to join him for a ménage at the Club.

"No proper gentleman sends a woman a butt plug as an invitation to a seedy club instead of roses."

"I'm not looking for a gentleman, Meemee." *I want Sully*. She wanted to be able to trust him not to walk out on her again. She wanted him to be the man she was looking for in her "A Hero Wanted" ad.

"Newsflash, girlfriend. White picket fence guys are gentlemen. Tell you the truth, I'm disappointed in Sully for not sending you roses. That's just not romantic. Maybe he's not the guy for you."

"Oh, cut the reverse psychology, Meems. It won't work. I know you want us back together."

Meemee smiled and rubbed her hands together.

"Okay, so what happened on the bar? Oh, jeez, don't tell me. Oh, God! Please do tell me."

"He went down on me."

Meemee's mouth dropped open in apparent shock. "On your first date?"

"It wasn't a date."

"Well then girlfriend that was some business trip. So are you going to wear it? Are you going to accept his invitation?"

Jenna picked up the plug. In the box, it had looked small but now, as she felt the weight in her hand, it seemed a little too big.

"Aha, a note!" Meems cried out. She snapped up a small piece of light blue paper from the box. "He says he wants to meet you in a week. At his bar, after closing. Wearing the plug. Are you going to do it?"

"I don't know, Meemee. What do you think?"

Meemee shook her head. "I'd hold off until he sent me roses."

Jenna rolled her eyes. "A lot of help you've turned out to be."

"I THINK SHE'S TAKEN the hook...er...I mean the plug," Meemee's cheerful voice echoed through the tiny, hot bar kitchen as Sully tried to balance two platters of chicken fingers in one hand and two platters of fries in the other.

Yes, the cook was back and, yes, he was threatening to quit again if Sully didn't get him help pronto. In an effort to stall the cook from walking out, Sully had thrown in to give him a hand tonight. Cripes! Was it his fault that the bar was growing leaps and bounds, and not one reliable person had applied for the cook's helper position?

"Hello! Sully! Did you hear me?" Meemee cried out as she sidestepped the angry, red-faced cook and followed Sully out of the kitchen into the noisy bar.

"Sorry, Meems, it's a bit hectic around here tonight. You really think Jenna is going to wear it?" Doubts had been circling ever since he'd sent that package off with Meemee. He still couldn't get over the fact that Jenna had allowed him to go down on her the other night. Things were happening a hell of a lot quicker than he'd thought they would.

Jenna *had* changed. Had become more at ease with her sexuality, and it just seemed to make her that much more attractive to him.

She'd been so sweet and succulent when he'd sucked her pussy juices into his mouth. The taste of her had just about driven him wild. Now he wanted more from her. A hell of a lot more. He just hoped he was doing the right thing in pushing her so fast. But it was the Club's rules to move swiftly on a woman. Not to allow her too much time to think or react with her brain but to instead respond with her body.

"You don't sound too happy. Don't tell me you're actually nervous about your next meeting with Jenna?" She giggled from behind him as he settled the plates in front of his customers.

"Nothing has really happened between Jenna and myself, Meems. Why are you so damned cheerful?" he asked as he headed back to the kitchen for yet another order.

"Because life is beautiful, my young apprentice. Especially when I see my uptight best friend finally melting in her attitude toward you."

Jenna was melting? Sully closed his eyes and said a silent thank you.

"Now we'll just have to wait and see if she shows for your meeting," Meemee continued. "When she does, then we move quickly on to the next phase. Have you got it all planned?"

"I do."

"Good..." She made a move to go but turned around again, her facial expression anything but happy.

"Sully?"

"Yeah?"

"No contact with her for the next week before Initiation. We want her all primed and eager for you."

"I know the rules, Meems."

She nodded. "Great stuff. Oh! And congratulations. You're already halfway into the Ménage Club. Because of the plug, she's aware of your intentions. Now all we've gotta do is persuade Jenna to join you for that one, hot Initiation night. I'm sure she'll not only go for it but she'll enjoy it as well."

"You think so?"

Meemee sighed wearily. "Those doubts are showing again, Sully. You've got one week to work on that problem, okay? You're going to have to be certain that this is the way you want to go."

"It is the way. I don't want to lose her this time around." Or ever.

"You stick to the plan and she'll thank you forever. Trust me—once she's Initiated, there won't be any looking back for her or for you."

He could hear the smile in Meemee's voice and nodded in agreement.

Yes, Meemee was right. Once Jenna accepted the invitation to be initiated into the Ménage Club then she would be his to pleasure.

His to pleasure forever.

Chapter Four

One week later...

"THE WAY SHE KEEPS TWIRLING her fingers through her hair makes me think she's a little bit unsure of herself," Tony said as he watched Jenna where she sat in a far corner booth while Sully, at Tony's request, mixed a banana daiquiri for the cute little redhead sitting alone at the end of the bar. Thankfully, Tony wasn't drinking himself. Last week when he'd gotten Tony out of jail, he'd made his friend promise not to get drunk and cause a disturbance every time he saw a redhead. Hopefully, Tony would hang onto his promise—at least for tonight.

"It's natural for her to be that way," Tony continued. "There's that trust barrier to break through. From everything you've told me about your relationship in the past, I'd say she's most likely afraid you'll leave town if you have another fight. And like she's said many times during your fights, she's afraid you'll leave her for some skinny chick, maybe even one of those endless ladies who you call friends."

"They *are* just friends, Tony."

"I know it, but she still doesn't believe it. You told me yourself she seemed pissed off when one of our Club members flirted with you right here at the bar the other week. Anyway, I'd be worried if she wasn't nervous. This indicates she's interested in getting back together with you, to make things right between you two, but she still has insecurities." At Tony's words, a memory zipped through Sully.

A memory of the summer he'd come to stay with his grandparents. Initially he'd come to help them with their bakery during the busy tourist season and to ponder on whether he should join NASA's new training program with his three cousins. Meemee and Tony also worked at the bakery. The three of them had become fast friends. It had been at Tony's twenty-first birthday bash when he'd first seen plus-sized Jenna. The instant he'd walked into Tony's apartment he'd been floored. Her adorable, wide blue eyes, sassy auburn curls and her shy, yet sexy smile had made his cock and the rest of him take immediate notice. He'd always been attracted to plus-sized women and he'd made it a point to get introduced to her. She'd seemed surprised when he'd quickly invited her out for coffee with Tony and Meemee after the party, and he'd been thrilled when she'd accepted.

Tony, Meemee, Jenna and himself had been inseparable that summer. Not a day went by that the four of them didn't get together for some reason or another. And not a day went by that he didn't have the urge to find out everything about Jenna MacLean. He also found himself wanting to kiss her soft-looking, cupid-shaped, luscious, ruby-red lips, or do naughty things to her plump, sweet-smelling body. Delicious things he'd heard his cousins' brag they did with their girlfriends. It hadn't taken him long to figure out Jenna was sexually shy. The moment he'd met her grandparents he'd known why. Her grandmother had been strict, religious and controlled Jenna's every move.

No wonder she had hang-ups.

Jenna's mother and father had been killed in a car crash when she'd only been two years old and her grandparents had taken over raising her. They'd imposed curfews on her, had made her quite uptight sexually. But with Meemee's help, Jenna had been able to go out often, under the guise that she and Meemee went to the movies or to the fair or shopping. That's when he'd hook up with Jenna and they'd go off by themselves.

Kissing her had been torturous—guilt had always brewed in her eyes afterwards. It had been frustrating to say the least, but he loved Jenna MacLean and he could be patient as hell. He'd vowed he would wait until she was ready. He'd wined her and dined her that summer, introduced her to his grandparents, who'd absolutely fallen in love with her during the fun Sunday dinners his grandmother loved to throw.

One hot summer night as they'd walked arm in arm down along the sandy beach watching the moonlight sparkle off the ocean's whitecaps they'd gone further than just kissing. Their touches had turned hungry. Desperate. Frantic.

They'd both been so turned on and she'd asked him to fuck her right then and there. It hadn't been the romantic way he'd planned to make love to her for her first time but he just hadn't been able to refuse that hungry, passionate look in her eyes or the delicious way her feminine fingers had shyly slipped into his pants and explored his cock.

Thank God, he'd had a condom in his wallet.

They'd consummated their relationship in a secluded grassy area near the beach's park gazebo beneath the twinkling stars. His heart had soared as he'd unleashed the passion from her, and made her orgasm. Unfortunately, after their lovemaking session and many more after that night, he'd seen guilt and shame shine bright in her eyes. Guilt and shame that her religious grandmother had no doubt instilled in her. Because of her guilt, he'd become angry. They'd fought frequently.

They'd also fought because he had quite a few friends who also happened to be women. She'd told him it wasn't proper for him to have so many women friends. In other words, she didn't trust him. Didn't believe him when he said he loved her and wanted only her in his life.

Frustration had begun to gnaw at him.

He'd even given her a vibrator. He'd figured it would help her explore her own body, her sexuality.

Toward the end of summer, her grandmother had found the sex toy and had freaked-out. Jenna had been in tears the last time he'd seen her. They'd had the big fight that night. She'd told him it wasn't proper for a man and woman to use sex toys.

It had just been too much. Bitterness and frustration had overwhelmed him and he'd told her he was leaving town. He'd sworn to her he'd never come back to Hideaway or come back to her. He'd left town with Tony and joined NASA's new training program.

That's why the advertisement Meemee had written on the napkin on behalf of Jenna had come as such a shock.

Anal. Sexually adventurous. Ménages. And not an ounce of that guilt he'd come to hate so much had sparked Jenna's eyes when he'd read the ad and looked at her. Where once there had been shyness, there was now hunger. Where there once had been hesitancy, there was now a refreshing boldness.

Shit! Her heated looks and the ad had turned him on so bad he'd needed to take several cold showers since then.

Sending her the butt plug had been a bold move. A test to make sure she would come here tonight. To prove to himself she really had changed. To ask her a question that could change their lives and hopefully bring them back together again.

And here she was. Near closing time. Casting shy, yet eager glances his way.

Did she have that inflatable butt plug buried up her cute little ass as he'd asked her to wear? Or was she here to tell him to take the plug and shove it up his own ass?

"I remember her being quite the innocent," Tony said as he lugged back a root beer. "Her grandmother made her that way. The old bitch sure had sexual hang-ups. It was a wonder she'd even let her husband near her to have a kid of her own."

"Don't speak ill of the dead, Tony," Sully teased, then walked the few steps to deliver the banana daiquiri to the redhead, who accepted the drink with a smile. She nodded her thanks to Tony, as well, and sent Sully back to him with an answer.

"So what did she say?" Tony eagerly asked when Sully returned.

"She said thanks but no thanks. She's not into men."

"Shit!" Tony said softly. "Another wasted drink."

Tony's gaze swung to Jenna again.

"With Jenna's grandmother out of the way, I wonder how much she's changed?"

"How do you mean?" Sully poured another beer for yet another waiting customer and pretended not to know what Tony meant.

"I mean, has she dropped her sexual shield? By the way she's squirming around on that bar seat, I'd say she's over her shyness and she's got that butt plug buried up there, making her pussy nice and tight. And the way her nipples are poking against her blouse makes me think the plug has turned her on, despite the intrusion up her sweet ass."

Sure enough, Tony was right. There was a cute blush to Jenna's cheeks, a sparkle in her eyes he'd never seen before.

"Sexually adventurous," Tony said again. "I'd even bet she's been fantasizing about a ménage. She's had a week to think about it."

Sully nodded his agreement. Jenna had mentioned light bondage in her ad. Mentioned ménages. But when it came right down to it, was she serious? Could he use her fantasies to get her to join the Ménage Club? Could he show her just how much he wanted her in his life?

He handed Tony another root beer and looked at his watch. Almost closing time. His gut twisted with anxiety. Soon he'd have his answer. One way or the other.

SHARDS OF SILVER RAIN were slapping against the windows of Sully's Bar & Grill when the last customer left.

Jenna was so nervous she almost left too.

Since shortly after she'd arrived, both Sully and Tony had been casting scorching glances her way. She didn't have to be a genius to know they'd been talking about her. Maybe even making plans for her?

Pushing her fingers anxiously through her hair, she watched Sully disappear into the back room.

After she'd received the sophisticated Ménage Club Initiation butt plug from Sully, she'd been plagued all that day by doubts. Should she try it? Should she send it back to him? By the end of the day, her brain had been fried from all that thinking, and finally excitement about trying it had prevailed. Later that night, she'd followed the directions. After turning the toy on, she'd watched how the plug had generously lubed itself.

Unbelievable technology!

The plug even felt contentedly warm, yet strange, as she'd inserted it slowly inside her. She'd gasped at the odd pleasure-pain as her firm muscles at first tried to reject the intrusion. But after relaxing herself and with some gentle prodding, her sphincter had given way and the toy slid in with fairly little pain after it having been so liberally self-lubed. To her surprise, the plug felt relatively comfortable as she'd worn it off and on over the next week. She'd scarcely even known it was there, had barely felt the gentle stretching motions as the plug had slowly but firmly inflated, gently massaging her anal muscles, prodding her wider—readying her.

Jenna blew out a breath and swallowed at the nervous tightness clogging up her throat. She'd missed Sully terribly over the past week. Had even picked up the phone many times to call him, but she'd persevered and each time she'd hung up.

Now she was here at Sully's Bar & Grill actually being turned on by the scorching way the two men were looking at her. Their hungry gazes made her feel desirable, sexy, and at the same time scared because she was actually fantasizing about having sex with Sully *and* Tony.

She'd be lying if she told anyone the thought of a ménage turned her off. It turned her on. Even if she and Sully never got together, she enjoy experimenting in a ménage à trois with him.

At the very least, her searing curiosity would be quenched...at the very worst, she'd become addicted to ménages...and isn't that what she'd heard the Ménage Club had been created to do? Make the intended couple become addicted to pleasuring each other long enough for them to stay together and work through their problems.

Oh, she'd heard the rumors. Heard about how the men and women at the Club captured their lovers through arousing their bodies. She had friends who swore ménages wouldn't work if the couple's relationship was in trouble. They said ménages were the ultimate trust factor between couples. That it should only be tried when a couple's relationship was clearly established because in some cases bringing a third into the bedroom broke a relationship.

Sully and she weren't even in a relationship so she really had nothing to lose if the idea was proposed. But what if Sully didn't propose the idea? Maybe she'd been misreading the signals those heated masculine looks had thrown her way? Maybe her instincts were just fantasy?

Jenna worried her bottom lip for a moment. No, her instincts were spot on with that butt plug he'd sent to her.

She'd been doing a lot of fantasizing since her grandfather and grandmother had died. As long as both of them had been alive, there had been some sort of unbreakable bond—a rope that kept her on the straight and narrow. Kept her from fulfilling her wickedly delicious sexual fantasies.

They'd passed away within weeks of each other. She'd grieved their loss for several months and, call it morbid, but after the grieving process had lifted, she'd felt liberated. A newfound guilty happiness had replaced the guilt of wanting sex with a man. With her strict, religious grandparents out of the way, she'd entered a new life and she'd begun dating men.

Begun experimenting with sex on a whole new level. But her sexual and emotional experiences with the local guys had always been lacking. It hadn't taken her too long to figure out she'd been comparing her men to Sully. Sully, her first man. The only man who'd made her orgasm.

"I think I'd like to join you in those carnal thoughts, Jenna."

Her head snapped up to find Sully standing over her, a heart-stopping grin on his face, and he was holding out his hand.

"Let's go for a walk."

"A walk? But it's raining out there."

"I know." He wiggled his fingers and without hesitation, she placed her hand against his firm palm.

Immediately he pulled her from the booth and against him. Shivers of excitement rippled through her as he pressed his hard bulge intimately against the juncture of her thighs. Her pussy clenched and she creamed. Tonight she'd purposely not worn underwear, eagerly anticipating a repeat performance of that gut-clenching oral session on the bar over a week ago.

"You look really nice in that dress, Jenna."

She tingled at his words. Tonight she'd opted to wear a cream-colored lace dress with a halter bodice, which accentuated her breasts, tied at the waist for shaping and a billowy skirt that flowed with her body as she walked.

"Come on, I've got a little surprise for you," he whispered softly. A beautiful smile lifted his lips and a sharp tug of warmth yanked at her heart.

"What are you up to?"

Suddenly everything about him seemed to intensify. His eyes became greener, his breathing faster.

"There's only one way for you to find out. Are you game?"

For a split second she hesitated. Instincts told her if she went with Sully Hero now, then there would be no turning back. She'd lose her heart to him all over again.

She thought about saying no. That she wasn't game for whatever he had in mind for her.

"I'm game," she whispered. Desperation and curiosity made her give in and she allowed him to lead her down the hallway.

At the back door, he pulled a thick green sweater off a hook.

"You're going to want to wear this, it'll get chilly where we're going." She slipped her arms into the sleeves of the sweater. The material felt warm and snug as it wrapped around her. It smelled of Sully and it felt as if he were embracing her.

He removed an umbrella from a stand and once they were out the back door, he popped the umbrella over them. It wasn't much protection from the warm spray of the late spring rain that slapped her face as he led her down the dark alley. The rain did nothing to cool the heated excitement building inside her as Sully and she walked across the secluded street and into the local park that hugged the ocean beach where they'd first made love.

In the distance, she noticed the white gazebo near the beach edge. It was well-lit, twinkling with pretty, white miniature lights indicating something was going on at this late hour. Maybe a party in the rain?

She drew her attention to Sully.

Silver raindrops glistened on his tanned arms, beaded his sexy five o'clock shadow, and landed on his full lips. Her nipples pulsed at the sight, remembering how wonderful his mouth had felt on her breasts when he'd suckled her in her shop. Her pussy trembled as she remembered the scorching touch of his mouth suckling her clit, licking her pussy lips, his tongue dipping into her vagina.

Suddenly he let go of her hand and turned to her.

She gasped as he dropped the umbrella and the rain came down on her, the unexpected wetness took her breath away. Without warning, his large fingers speared themselves into her tangled hair and he eased her head backward, exposing her lips for him. Hard heat from his body slammed into her as he pulled her against him.

"Jenna," he whispered. His hot breath caressed the cool raindrops on her lips as he brushed his warm mouth ever so slightly against hers.

The erotic touch made her knees weaken and she reached up and wrapped her arms around his neck. He groaned as she pulled gently on the wet strands of his short hair.

Oh, yes, she'd missed this. Missed touching him, being close to him, feeling safe and loved in his arms. She missed the sexy, masculine scent of man that was so distinct and unique to him.

"Widen your legs for me, Jenna."

Her head spun as she did what he wanted. Her legs trembled and she moaned softly as his warm fingers slipped up her dress and glided along the insides of her thighs.

He touched her labia, tenderly circled her clit until she was breathing harshly. Then he touched the plug.

"You wore it." Surprise laced his voice.

"Yes," she whispered.

"You understand what wearing the plug means? That you've agreed to be initiated into the Ménage Club? That afterwards you'll be asked to make a commitment to the Club and to me?"

Oh, sweet mercy, he was actually talking the commitment word, even after they had been apart for so long.

She nodded, pushed her lower half closer to his stroking fingers.

"Despite the Club, you're mine, Jenna. No matter who else takes you, understand?"

She understood what he was saying. He would be bringing her to that exclusive club where she would be expected to be intimate with a third.

"But first we need to talk," he said.

Frustration grabbed her as he pulled away. Once again he clutched her hand, his hot palm seared into hers.

"Sully?" What the hell was going on?

"Let's go see the surprise I have for you."

Shit! She thought his touching her, fucking her in the park in the rain would be the surprise.

He settled the umbrella over them again and led her down the path, all the while his masculine smell mingled with the fragrance of rain. The dual scents wrapped around her creating tension in her pussy.

Through the silvery rain, she noticed that well-lit gazebo again. As they drew closer, she could hear the buoys clanging out on the water and the ocean waves crashing over the nearby sandy beach.

Was this the surprise? Making love in a gazebo that overlooked the ocean beach where they'd first consummated their relationship?

That certainly would be romantic. They were also walking in the rain. Both were prerequisites for the hero she was looking for in her napkin ad.

Her heart picked up a mad tempo when they stepped up the wooden stairs, out of the rain, and walked into the windowless structure. She stopped short at the tiny, intimate table for two placed in the middle of the gazebo. The table setting looked absolutely gorgeous splashed with silver cutlery and a bright red tablecloth. In the middle sat a bottle of pink bubbly and beside it a clear crystal vase laden with ruby-red tulips.

She swallowed. Red tulips were her favorite flowers.

"Oh my gosh, what's this?"

"It looks like some couple is getting pretty romantic," Sully whispered as he pressed against her backside and snapped the umbrella closed. Rain poured past the gazebo openings in dripping sheets and echoed noisily on the roof.

They were isolated and in an intimate setting. From here, she could visualize the dark patch of grass hugging the beach, mere feet away, where they'd made love for the first time.

It brought back a rush of memories. Of their naked bodies intertwined beneath the summer moonlight. Her cry of pain when he'd first entered her, the wickedly delicious sensations that had followed.

She also remembered their fights and it suddenly made her feel very unsure of herself. Maybe she'd made a mistake by coming here? Maybe things couldn't be worked out between them?

"We should get out of here before the couple comes back," she whispered.

She made a move to go but his fingers intertwined with hers, holding her firm. "No need to run. The couple is already here."

Shoot! Why did she know he was going to say that?

"Sully—"

"Shhh, let's just eat and talk."

That's the last thing she wanted to do right now. Part of her wanted to run away, part of her wanted to stay and ask him to do naughty things to her... Heck, her mind was twisting with confusing thoughts. Had he forgotten about the butt plug buried in her ass? Had he forgotten what had happened between them in the past?

He slid out a chair and gestured for her to sit. Suddenly he looked way too serious and fear dashed through her. Now that it was finally happening—that Sully was finally going to talk about them—she was unsure of what she wanted.

Did she want to join the Ménage Club? Did she want another man touching her? Did Sully want that? Would a third person in their relationship actually help get them together? Could something so controversial as the Ménage Club actually work and get them *and* keep them together?

With all those questions fluttering around in her head, her brain said "absolutely not". Joining a club was not the answer. On the other hand, her heart and her body were saying something totally the opposite.

Yes, she wanted to learn to trust Sully. Yes, she wanted to try ménages with him. And what better way for her to learn to trust him again than by having a third in their bedroom? Gosh, it sounded so crazy that it just might work!

Then there was that one hundred percent success rate she'd heard about.

"This all seems so...extreme for me," she admitted, feeling overwhelmed that Sully Hero was actually talking to *her* about reigniting their relationship.

"Just hear me out, Jenna. If you don't like what I have to propose, you can walk."

She nodded and sat down, the butt plug pushing up her behind, reminding her of what she'd agreed to do just by wearing it and coming here.

Beneath the table, she intertwined her fingers nervously.

"You said we'd talk, so talk."

"Let's eat first." He made a grab for the chilling champagne bottle.

"No, Sully. You talk or I walk." There was no way she was going to fall for this romantic dinner. She needed to hear his proposition. Needed to make herself believe she wasn't dreaming.

"Okay, but first let's have some champagne."

"You're stalling, Sully."

He smiled. God! He looked so damn sexy, with his hair all wet and curly, as if he'd just stepped out of the shower and his hand... She watched his long fingers wrap around the bottle of pink champagne and imagined him touching her, parting her pussy lips, his head lowering between her legs as he'd done back at the bar last week. Jenna stifled a moan and swallowed at the carnal flutter rippling through her lower belly.

He filled both their goblets and handed her one.

"A toast. To pink champagne and romantic red tulips." His eyes were dark and sparkled with lust and something else... Hope?

A voice of reason told her to get the hell out of there before she entered a world of ménages. A world she knew nothing about. Instead, she clinked her glass against his then sipped the sweet, cool liquid.

Very nice. She sipped some more. The bubbles burst against her tongue with wonderful explosions and she closed her eyes, enjoying the fruity palate. She could already feel the alcohol warming her blood, making her flush. Champagne always did that to her, even with just a few simple sips.

"Let's see what kind of food we have for our dinner, shall we?"

More stalling!

"Sully..."

He lifted the elegant silver lid holding her plate hostage and she gasped in surprise at the luscious-looking, steaming hamburger, fries and a sprig of decorative parsley.

"No way," she said, shaking her head with surprise.

"What? You expected something else?" He sounded hurt, but amusement played in his eyes.

"Anything but your grandmother's famous burgers and fries." Another favorite of hers. When Jenna and Sully had gone out together, having dinner at Sully's grandparents every Sunday was a fun time. His grandmother always made delicious burgers, fries and salads.

He folded his muscular arms over his wet shirt, illuminating his nipples beneath the wet cloth. Oh boy. The erotic way those muscles played as he moved made a dangerous wave of desire race through her.

Rein it in, Jen. Rein it in.

That's when she realized where his lust-filled eyes had strayed to.

She looked down and realized she hadn't buttoned the sweater. It hung wide open, revealing her own damp clothing hugging the generous curves of her breasts. Her peaked nipples were also outlined, special thanks to the rain that had whipped against them earlier when he'd lowered the umbrella. She hadn't worn a bra tonight, had wanted to make it easier for his hands to touch her, so he was getting a real eyeful.

Her face warmed at the sight of her large nipples pressing against the cream-colored dress—she could even see the dark outline of her areolas.

She should be over this shy bit with Sully, shouldn't she? She wanted him. He obviously wanted her. So why was she feeling...embarrassed?

"I'm starved," he said. His voice sounded low, husky and seductive as if he were saying he was starving for her, not food. To her disappointment, he picked up his burger and started munching away.

This time it was her turn to watch him. To stare at the scrumptious way his lips wrapped around the burger, the seductive way the tips of his mouth curled upward as he smiled at the taste of it, obviously enjoying the robust flavor.

Her tummy growled.

He laughed.

"Come on, eat. Why are you so tense? I won't do anything you don't want me to do."

Great! How was she supposed to eat after he said something like that?

Her stomach growled again.

Sully lifted an eyebrow. "Are you going to eat? Or do I have to feed you myself?"

Oh wouldn't that go over well, having his long, luscious fingers touching her mouth as he finger-fed her bits of burger and fries. She wanted to have his fingers in her mouth, her sucking his fingertips, licking the taste of him from her lips.

Oh boy.

His eyes twinkled darker with amusement.

She picked up her burger and started eating. Flavor she remembered so well slammed against her taste buds and she moaned her gratitude.

"Nice sound," he whispered. "You should do it more often."

"Shut up, Hero, and eat your food."

And that's what they did. They devoured the food Sully's grandmother had prepared for them and, to her surprise, it felt as if she were sinking right back into old times. Chatting with Sully, finding out about his astronaut training, digging around for information on any girls he'd dated in between assignments while he'd been gone. His playful avoidance of her questions about those girls seemed, oddly enough...reassuring and relaxing, and even enjoyable—that he'd taken her feelings into consideration and not talked about them. It allowed the same familiar roar of sexual tension to hum all around them that had been there years ago during their time together.

As he related his experience with NASA, she noticed his sudden frown.

"And then NASA asked us if we might be interested in a top secret assignment. My cousins, you remember them, Joe, Ben and Buck...were totally gung ho about it. I wasn't."

"I find that hard to believe. I know you were thinking of joining the team when we first met. Your desire to go out into space. Why'd you change your mind? Why did you come back here?" That last sentence slipped out even before she realized she'd been thinking it out loud.

Sully sighed. It was a ragged, uneven breath of frustration. The sound squeezed her heart and made her burst with pain for him. Obviously, his space adventures hadn't turned out the way he'd thought.

"Have you ever left something behind and then later realized it was the most important thing in your life?"

She'd realized what she'd lost when Sully had left town and because of the pain she now experienced at his sigh, she wasn't sure how to respond, so she remained silent.

"It's because I left you behind that I realized how important you are to me, Jenna."

Oh. Wow. This was something she'd craved to hear, and now that he was actually saying it, she couldn't believe she wasn't seriously dreaming. She resisted the impulse to pinch herself.

"You've heard about the Ménage Club," he said. It was an unexpected statement, not a question. Surprise almost made her choke on her food at how quickly he'd broached the subject, but she managed to gulp it down before he noticed her reaction.

"Yes, about how it brings estranged couples back together—" she swallowed at her nervousness "—with the help of a third and sometimes a fourth."

She managed to act nonchalant, as if what they were discussing was an everyday occurrence to her. To her satisfaction, she even managed to take another bite of her burger despite the wild pounding of her heart beating against her chest.

"I know what we had together could be classified as a summer fling."

A summer fling? Was that all she'd been to him?

"But for me it was more than that."

"For me too," she admitted.

The tips of his mouth turned upward at her confession.

"And we have this overwhelming sexual attraction that has stayed with us over the years."

"But a relationship can't be based on sexual attraction alone," she voiced, hoping he felt the same way.

"I realize that we've got a lot of work to do, and the way we left it between us... It shouldn't have happened that way. I apologize. I shouldn't have let my anger blind me toward my love for you and it isn't a love based on sex."

"I know. There's something else between us. Even though we fought, we always seemed to get back together...except for that last one. I'm to blame too. Don't you see? It was my upbringing. I was tied too much to my grandparents. They were both very strict with me... You have to understand—" she took a deep breath and continued "—and I kept thinking you were fooling around on me with all those women friends of yours."

"I wasn't. I still have those women friends, though. I won't get rid of them just because of your insecurities. They are friends, and that's all they'll ever be."

The flare of anger reared its ugly head again, but it quickly disappeared at his next words.

"I came back to Hideaway for you, Jenna. I wanted to come back sooner, but I had a contract to fill and I was out of this world...literally." He grinned. "I was halfway across the galaxy when I realized being an astronaut wasn't for me. I realized not having you in my life wasn't for me."

His confession made a wave of warm happiness spill through her but they still had so much to work through.

"There's something you should know..." Since he was being honest, she may as well be too. "Because of what happened, because of the way you left... I can't trust you not to do it again. How do I know that with our first fight or some disagreement down the line, you won't leave me?"

"I was young and immature back then, Jenna. I'm a man now. A man with responsibilities, a business... Maybe I'm not the white picket fence kind of guy like you want, but I know that I want you, Jenna. I want you to learn to trust me again. I want to make you happy and, as crazy as it sounds, I want our relationship to start off on a sound footing. Our past pattern hasn't been very good so I went looking for help from the Ménage Club. Meemee said it would work—"

"Meemee! You based your decision on Meems? She doesn't know anything about the Club or ménages for that matter." Did she?

"She's in it, Jenna. She's one of the instructors."

She blinked as both shock and hurt knifed through her.

Her best friend was a part of the notorious club and she hadn't told her? She should be more upset than this, shouldn't she?

"The Initiation is tonight, Jenna. One night of pleasuring you with a couple of others from the Club. No strings. After that, we can talk again. If you want to walk, then you can walk. But, Jenna, know that I can't go back to the way it was between us. I can't fight with you anymore when you get angry with me. I won't, because I can't hurt you again as I did in the past. It would kill me this time around. So? Are you in?"

He held out his hand to her.

His hand resembled a bond. A bond she never wanted to break with him.

She nodded as she placed her hand into Sully's outstretched one.

"I'm in."

Chapter Five

"MEEMEE! I AM GOING to kill you!" Jenna spat at her best friend. It was a mere few minutes later and Sully had dropped her off at Meemee's place, but not before giving her a searing kiss, which reminded Jenna of exactly why she wanted Sully back in her life.

Now she stood with her friend inside a closed lingerie store down the street from Meemee's apartment. Apparently, the Ménage Club had given Meems a key to this place and instructed her to help Jenna get ready for her Initiation.

"What did I do now?" Meems asked as her hands scrambled between a shimmering blue chemise and some skimpy red outfit.

"You never told me you belonged to the Club," Jenna hissed as she stood beside Meemee. Jenna wore nothing but her thong and a warm terrycloth towel Meemee had given her after instructing her to take off all her damp clothing in the store. She didn't feel the least bit self-conscious or embarrassed at having Meemee seeing her partially nude or totally naked for that matter. They'd seen each other in their birthday suits off and on ever since they'd decided to be best friends in kindergarten.

"So? You never told me Sully was so well-hung either," she giggled.

"Meemee, please be serious. Why didn't you ever tell me? Why the big secret? We're supposed to be best friends. We're supposed to share everything."

Meemee turned from the rack of sexy clothing and winked at her. "Even best friends have secrets, sweetie. Now how about this outfit? It's a hot red, baby doll satin and lace with open bust and strapless, and it's cute with these frilly ribbons and it's crotchless... Your face isn't giving me the 'okay, this is a great outfit' signal... What's the matter? Have you changed your mind about the Club?"

Sweet heavens! No! She'd never been so excited in her life! Just thinking about actually having sex with Sully along with others participating—not to mention the Club's unbeatable success rate—how could she even think about changing her mind?

"It's not sexy enough. Besides I don't think I look so great in red."

"Hmm, okay, give me an idea of what you're looking for," she said as she chewed her lower lip thoughtfully.

"I want something daring," Jenna admitted. Her heart was thumping a mile a minute at what she envisioned herself wearing. "Something that Sully won't expect. Something that will blow Sully's mind...and get him so horny he wants to take me right there and then. Something that will complement my figure."

"Newsflash, Jen. He wants you no matter what you look like." She threw the red outfit back onto the rack and turned to Jenna, a scolding tone to her voice. "Woman! He is in love with you! L-o-v-e! Or haven't you figured that out yet? Why the hell do you think he came back to Hideaway? Why would he join the Club? Why would he agree to this Initiation? He's not willing to go the regular route of trying to get back together with you because it's failed in the past. During your relationship, you guys broke up so many times it had my head spinning. I can only imagine how he felt or you, for that matter. Am I not right? You two kept getting back together and just kept on fighting and breaking apart again."

"Yes, but—" She wanted to tell Meems that Sully had already told her all this and that she eagerly looked forward to what was going to happen tonight, but her friend seemed to be on a roll, and when she wanted to get her point across, she wouldn't stop talking until she had her say.

"He knows you both have problems that don't have an easy fix. Sure, maybe relationship counseling might help your jealousy issue about him being so hunky gorgeous. And it might help your problem that you don't feel as if you deserve such a good-looking guy, even if you aren't svelte and drop-dead gorgeous like those thin, anorexic models in those lousy glam-glam magazines. But, Jenna, our way at the Club proves that everyone is equal. Fat, skinny, short or tall, we all want to be loved, and to have sex and be pleasured without feeling guilty about our sexuality or whatever the hell problem some couple is working on. The way they do it at the Club is a hell of a lot quicker in helping to repair a relationship than traditional counseling. And it's a lot more fun. Ménages, when used right, are the ultimate trust factor in a relationship. Are you getting my meaning?"

"Think sexy, Meems. Sexy, hot, something flattering. What do you wear to the Ménage Club when you want to grab a man's attention?"

Jenna hid a smile as Meemee emitted a frustrated curse. "Haven't you been listening to me? He doesn't care what you look like—"

"Every word, Meems. Now move aside so I can see what else is on this rack. I have a man to catch."

SULLY'S HEART WAS POUNDING a mile a minute as he stepped out of the shower adjoining the lavish bedroom they'd be using at the Ménage Club, which was actually in the basement of Tony's secluded, beachfront, three-story home a few miles outside Hideaway, Maine.

"You're looking more nervous than a virgin bridegroom on his wedding night," Tony chuckled from the doorway.

"In a way I am, aren't I?" Sully said as he grabbed a towel and began to dry himself, being extra careful around his rock-hard cock. "It's been years since I've made love to her. I've almost defied the Club rules several times and shown her how much I want her back."

"But you didn't defy us and now, tonight, you will show her what she'll have in store for the rest of her life...if she so chooses to accept the rules of the Club."

"It's been killing me not to be intimate with her, Tony. I mean intimate the old-fashioned way...one-on-one."

Tony's expression softened. "All in good time, Sully. All in good time. I know it's been hard staying away from Jenna. When a man is in love with a woman, he wants to express it by making love to her, but that would have repeated your old pattern."

Tony was right. Sully knew it, but it didn't mean he could easily turn off the way he was raised. His mother had always told him that love between a man and a woman would solve all problems. Too bad she'd been wrong in this case.

Sometimes outside help, no matter how extreme, was needed to repair a relationship and regain the trust of the woman he loved.

"Here's a little something to keep you going for Jenna. It's state of the art. New on the market," Tony said as he placed something on the bathroom counter.

Sully's eyes widened and his cock immediately pulsed as he recognized the item he'd seen advertised on the Net and had been meaning to get. He blew out a breath as he examined the supple leather item and the bronze ring. He knew full well he'd need the help of this device because without it, he was so hot and horny, he just might explode before Jenna was ready for him.

"Thanks, Tony. I appreciate it."

"Hey, what else are best friends for?"

"SHIT, MEEMS. I'M GETTING nervous," Jenna admitted as Meemee ushered her down the elaborate marble staircase that led to Tony's basement. She'd never been to his beach house, or maybe castle was a better word for it. She'd never realized such an extravagant house actually existed so close to the pretty little tourist town of Hideaway. Tony had built both it and the Club a couple of years ago when he'd come back from one of his astronaut missions. She'd been invited for the housewarming but had to decline because she'd been busy getting her antiques shop in working order.

And now, here she was...under totally different circumstances. Totally erotic circumstances.

She couldn't believe this was actually happening. She was actually going through with this Initiation.

Sweet mercy! Had she flipped her lid? Was she so desperate she'd try anything to be with Sully? Or was she finally loosening up and letting her true sensual nature shine through?

"Girl, I'd be nervous too."

At her friend's words, her nervousness only increased. "Gee, thanks for helping."

"C'mon, Jen, I'm joking. There's no need to be anxious. You'll be fine, and remember Sully will be with you every step of the way."

Strangely enough, having her say that, actually calmed her a bit.

"Thanks, Meems."

"Hey! What else are best friends for?"

Suddenly Jenna realized she'd been focused so much on herself tonight she hadn't even realized when Sully had dropped her off at Meemee's that her friend was dressed in a flirty, one-shouldered minidress with a keyhole bodice and buckle trim. The midnight blue dress contrasted so beautifully with her long, straight blonde hair that the familiar tinge of wanting to have the same perfect body as Meemee's crept into her mind.

Jenna shoved her envy aside. No use wanting to be someone else. She needed to stay comfortable in her own skin. That's where her happiness lay.

That, however, didn't stop the guilt from sweeping in around her. "I ruined your evening, didn't I, Meems?"

Meemee looked surprised and shook her head. "Ruined my evening? What makes you say that?"

"You're dressed to kill and now you're bringing me over here to Tony's, so I'm making you late for your date."

"I always dress this way when I come to the Club."

Dressing for Tony perhaps? Tony was an idiot if he hadn't noticed Meems by now, and joining a club just so she could be with Tony was kind of stupid, wasn't it?

Jenna stifled a laugh at that thought. She was doing the same thing just to be with Sully so who was she to cast stones?

"Which reminds me, best friends aren't supposed to have secrets. Why didn't you tell me you joined the Club?" Focusing on her friend might take her mind off what would be happening soon. Unfortunately, Meemee wasn't in the mood for talking about herself.

"This is the bedroom you'll be using," she whispered as she grabbed Jenna by the hand and giggled as she pushed the oak door open to present the awesome sight.

"Oh!" was all Jenna could say as she surveyed the bedroom suite decorated in misty blue and gold highlights. In the middle of the room was a wrought iron canopy bed where a fluffy blue and white square comforter was folded back to reveal midnight-blue satiny sheets and matching pillows.

The walls were virgin white with gorgeous, tastefully framed pictures of nude sex scenes, most of them shots of group sex that made Jenna's pulse race with both excitement and a tinge of anxiety. Perfectly normal under these conditions. Especially when she was going into a world she didn't know too much about except for what she'd researched on the Net and that was totally different than what she would be experiencing tonight.

She was glad she wore the sparkling, white leather chemise with lace trimming at the half-cups and hem. It made her fit right into this gorgeous, sexy scene. The instant Jenna had spied the outfit, she'd known it was what she'd wanted. It hugged her plus-size figure to perfection, the underwire cups cradled her large breasts, allowing ample cleavage, and the material dropped over her rounded belly, hiding it nicely.

The clothing gave her a sexy, flirty, feminine kind of feeling and that's what she wanted for Sully. It also had a provocative slit that went right up her sides, giving a great view of her bare legs and hips, allowing the men to realize she wore no underwear, making herself easily accessible.

She'd removed the plug as per Meemee's instructions and her ass now throbbed and ached to be filled again.

Jenna swallowed against a flutter of nerves as the lights suddenly dimmed and soft, romantic music floated through the room. Behind her, the door softly clicked shut.

She turned around and discovered Meemee gone.

Some best friend! Deserting her in her hour of need. She made a move to follow Meemee when nearby another door she hadn't noticed opened.

Jenna did a double take as Sully strolled into the room. He wore a two-tone charmeuse robe, dark forest green accented with emerald green. The coloring of his robe enhanced the green hunger in his eyes as he saw her standing there.

"Jenna, I'm glad you could make it," he whispered as he came toward her. His hair was damp, curling wildly, and made him look so damn sexy that for a split second she thought she just might be having an erotic dream about him.

His eyes shone brightly with desire, hunger splashed across his handsome face. The sexy way his nostrils flared as he caught the scent of his favorite perfume she'd dabbed behind her ears had her own breath backing up in her lungs and her physically backing up as well. She hadn't even realized she'd been so overwhelmed by the erotic sensations spiraling through her that she'd backed into the door, the coolness of the oak smacking against her bottom.

"I've waited a long time for us, Jenna. A long time to finally be with you."

"Me too," she whispered, reacting to his touch as his hands came to settle at her elbows.

His fingers slid with featherlike strokes along the sides of her arms and awareness coursed through her.

"Are you sure you want this?" he asked. She could see the need to be with her so clearly now as he looked into her eyes.

She nodded, suddenly unable to speak, mesmerized by the tingling sensations sifting up along her arms as he continued to stroke her flesh.

"You look absolutely beautiful in that outfit." His words warmed her, his soft touches set her on fire.

"Thank you." She'd never been much for compliments, but his always made her feel so nice.

"They've given us a little time together. Time to get to know one another a little more intimately."

His hand dropped down to brush her wrist. Erotic sensations spiraled through her at the intimate caress. Lacing her fingers with his, he led her to the bed.

He kneeled on the mattress and climbed on. She followed suit, finding the mattress soft and welcoming beneath her hands and feet.

"Come closer. Onto your knees. In front of me," he said softly. She couldn't believe she was actually shivering with so much anticipation as she did what he asked. Nothing had even happened yet and there she was trembling like a freaking virgin on her wedding night. In a way she was, wasn't she? She hadn't made love with Sully in years.

She inhaled sharply as he lifted his hands and speared his fingers through her hair. His touch was gentle, loving, and the sensations running through her scalp felt so...erotic.

"I've missed you so much, Jenna. Missed touching you. Loving you. Being with you."

"Me too," she whispered enjoying the sensual way he played with her hair.

"Touch me, Jenna."

Her fingers sifted through silk as she touched his scalp. He gave a primal growl. The sound made her heart pound with maddening speed.

"Do you see how your touch affects me, Jenna? You've always made me feel like no other woman has ever has."

At the mention of another woman she couldn't help but tense, the familiar pang of raw anger sifted to the surface. He noticed her reaction but said nothing. Instead, his fingers touched her scalp, massaging in soft, sensual circles that had her momentary anger melting away.

Suddenly she felt as if she were a nervous new mare in a stallion's harem. The stallion brushing against her, testing her willingness to mate, smelling her, wanting her, but also sensing he needed to go slow so as not to frighten her off.

"You will always be the only woman for me, Jenna. Even when I'm with others at the Ménage Club, you will be number one."

Why was he doing this to her? Why was he talking about other women when he knew it upset her so badly? Again that familiar raw anger she'd never cared for but couldn't seem to stop seeped through her. She felt an instantaneous need to bolt or, better yet, slap him for even thinking about other women when he was there with her.

"Shh, Jenna. Easy. Remember why we are here. This is how it will be if you join the Club, sweetie."

His masculine fingers were still stroking, trying to soothe her as he massaged her scalp in erotic little circles. Tender touches that sent delicious little tingles down the back of her neck and into her shoulders. Shoulders she hadn't even realized were tense.

"The Ménage Club deals with exposure therapy, Jenna. Exposing us to something that bothers us. Exposing ourselves over and over again until all our insecurities are gone and we are both immune to the thing we feared the most. Do you understand?"

She nodded, but damned if she wasn't still pissed off at him.

And getting just a wee bit turned on at the sensual way his fingers were now brushing the sides of her face and tracing her lips.

"Did you know that our mouths are one of the more sensitive parts of our body? Kissing someone combines three of our senses. Taste, touch and smell."

Jenna swallowed as he leaned closer. His green eyes were sexually charged, his lips parted slightly.

"You smell so good, Jenna. Sweet and sexy like my woman should smell."

Her heart thumped out of control as with the tenderest of touches he held her bottom lip while he kissed the sensitive inner curve between her neck and shoulder. The featherlight touch assaulted her senses.

"You're soft as velvet and you taste like candy—very addictive candy."

"Keep those compliments coming," she murmured as the familiar slow burn unraveled between her legs. She arched closer to him, allowing him to plant tiny erotic kisses along her collarbone until she was whimpering beneath the electrical sensations flaming through her.

This was one of the reasons she'd never been able to stay with a man for too long in relationships after Sully. None of them ever made her feel as he did. None of them could make the hot need for sex race through her veins like Sully could.

"Keep touching me," he whispered. "This Initiation is for both of us."

She blinked, suddenly realizing her hands were still tangled in his soft curls.

God! She'd been so selfish! Taking from him and not giving anything back.

Following his lead, she began her own technique of soft, little massages against his scalp that had his breath quickening just like hers.

She smiled at how easily he responded to her touch. How easily he radiated love when he looked at her. How easily he made her body ache for him.

Angling his head between her shoulder and neck she watched as he ran a pink tongue along the top of her shoulder, caressing her skin and leaving behind a trail of wet fire.

Jesus! That felt good!

He eased away from her. She found herself leaning toward him. Tasting his broad chest, kissing one of his puckered brown nipples. His breath caught and she shyly drew the tight bud into her mouth, gently laving it with her tongue, exploring the tiny ridges until the nub felt hard and hot inside her mouth.

"Jesus, Jenna."

His hands were on her shoulders, easing her sexy garment down her arms and over her waist, his fingers instantly heating everywhere he touched. She enjoyed the tingling sensations of his intimate caresses and could not stop herself from kissing the soft, damp curls on his broad chest and inhaling his intoxicating scent deep into her lungs.

He'd always smelled so manly. Tonight was no exception.

She hadn't even realized her breasts had burst free from her cups until his warm hands palmed them. Looking down, she found his thumbs rasping her nipples. Her thighs tightened in response. Her pussy clenched in wicked anticipation. She felt so hot and wet. So on fire. The incredible sensations made her moan.

"You sound so sexy when you make that noise, Jenna. I want to bring more of those sensual sounds out of you tonight. Every night."

His hands roamed over her breasts, exploring her generous curves, his thumbs moving rhythmically while his mouth locked over hers in carnal, possessive movements pushing more cries from her. He slid his tongue into her mouth, caressing her gums, avoiding her own eager tongue.

The avoidance only made her want him more.

Splaying her hands against his chest, she loved the way his damp, hot muscles moved beneath her fingertips. She slid her hands onto his hard, muscular shoulders and eased his robe off, allowing it to puddle around them on the bed.

He returned the favor and slid her chemise off her. She wiggled her legs and feet until it slipped onto the mattress.

"I'm going to make love to you like I've never done before, Jenna," he breathed against her lips. Then he was easing her down near the foot of the bed and close to the side edge. It was an oddly curious position and, before she could ask why she was being placed in this way, his succulent mouth fused with hers once again, the heat of his upper body washing intimately against her. His hands released her breasts and smoothed over her rounded belly curling into her belly ring. He pulled gently, just enough to bring an erotic chord of sensation shimmering through her tummy.

"I'm going to brand you tonight. Make you mine. Mark you for the Club," he said. As he moved closer, he sucked a nipple into his mouth. He wasn't gentle as he'd been in her antiques store. Instead, he was eager and harsh, his tongue moving in seductive swirls against her hardening bud.

"Oh, God!" She just about came off the bed as his sharp teeth suddenly nipped at her tender flesh and his fingers tweaked and plumped her other nipple.

He kissed the aching tip then sucked it into his mouth again. His tongue laved it, washing away the pleasure-pain. He did the same to her other nipple, nipping and laving, leaving her hot and bothered, pleasure washing through her. He lowered his lethal lips over her belly, making her clench her tummy muscles as he headed for parts south.

Her hips arched to him as he spread her legs and climbed in between them. His eyes were so dark and fierce she could barely breathe.

She'd expected him to go down on her, to dip his head between her legs and suckle her clit and pussy, but to her disappointment he didn't. Instead, she noticed something in his hand.

A vibrator! And straps dangled off it.

She swallowed as her mind exploded with delicious scenarios along with a touch of fear.

The vibrator was huge. Just as big, if not bigger than his cock.

"Just so you know, the vibrator is self-lubricating so I can use it in your sweet ass later."

Oh boy.

"Your pussy is so beautiful, Jenna," he whispered as he positioned himself between her widespread legs. "Flushed red like a tulip with luscious, silky petals waiting to be opened."

Wicked sensations tore through her as he touched her. His possessive fingers parted her labia, the warm head of the vibrator slid into her wet vagina. She fought for breath as the item filled her, stretched her, sank deep inside her. Closing her eyes, she moaned softly as the clitoris stimulator pressed snugly onto her aching flesh. A moment later soft straps went around her thighs holding the sex toy in place.

Instantly the toy began an erotic pulse, making her vagina clench and cream with heat. He was now sliding his hand up her right arm, his gaze holding her, mesmerizing her. His fingers tingled against her flesh. Curled around her wrist, bringing her arm above her head.

He kissed her on the nose, his eyes twinkling with arousal as he brought her other arm up over her head pinning both her wrists beneath one hand. Holding her there. Holding her captive.

Reaching above her head, he seemed to search for something beneath the covers.

"Sully?" She wanted to know what he had there, the curiosity burning her alive.

"Shh, don't talk. Just feel, Jenna. Let your mind soar. Let your body respond."

Something soft snapped around her wrist and then the other. She heard the clink of chain, knew instinctively he'd bound her.

Light bondage, just as she'd asked for in her "A Hero Wanted" ad.

"I love you, Jenna. Now I'm going to show you just how much."

Tears sprung to her eyes and joy shot through her heart. Sweet Jesus, she'd waited so long to hear him say those three words again. She wanted to tell him she loved him too when she felt the mattress near the top of her head move.

Someone had joined them!

She angled her head up and found Tony looking down at her. His straight white teeth flashed against his tanned face in a wide smile of approval. Lust gleamed in his dark brown eyes. She could swear her flesh tingled as his searing gaze raked along her naked length, taking in her plus-sized curves, her belly button ring and to the vibrator inside her pussy. "You did well, Sully. How are you feeling, Jenna?"

Aroused? Excited? Confused at being so eager to see Tony there with her?

All of the above?

"At a loss for words?" Tony chuckled. "Just relax, Jenna."

Relax! My God! Her breath was coming faster as she caught sight of his bare chest, naked abdomen and...

Tony's calloused palms shocked her flesh as they slid over her collarbone then slipped over her swollen breasts. His masculine fingers knew exactly where to touch her, how to squeeze her nipples in such a beautiful way that pleasure and pain mixed perfectly.

She looked down and saw Sully's eyes sparkle magnificently as he watched Tony touch her. Her breasts tingled beneath Tony's sensual massage and a line of arousal zipped from her nipples right down to her sex toy-filled pussy. In response, her quivering, wet vaginal muscles clenched tightly around the vibrator nestled deep inside her.

"Go ahead, Sully," Tony whispered.

Sully's Adam's apple bobbed up and down as he swallowed. He kept his eyes on her as his own breaths came through his open mouth in short, raspy gasps. In an erotic slowness that had her mesmerized, she watched Sully get off the mattress. He stood at the foot of the bed in front of her and unsnapped the side snaps. His thong loosened and fell away, making her eyes widen at the spectacular sight.

Sully's cock was already well-engorged and stiff with arousal. His mushroom-shaped head was fully released from its sheath, flushed purple with a dot of pre-come at the slit. But that's not what captured her immediate attention, though. What really gripped her and her soaked pussy was the fact Sully's cock was nestled in full bondage gear.

HE'D NEVER SEEN ANYTHING more erotic in his life. The woman he wanted with every breath of his being was splayed out in front of him, his best friend's hands roaming over her breasts like a seductive lover's, ripples of muscles clenched in her belly and a vibrator was tucked snugly inside her vagina keeping her on edge while he prepared for the next phase of their Initiation. The way her mouth was slightly parted as she panted harshly through her arousal had his cock pulsing against the restraints of the cock cage Tony had given him.

The leather cock strap was worn behind his balls with a divider strap that separated his scrotum enhancing his two perfectly shaped swollen spheres. The harness and divider were made of soft, supple black leather with a chrome cock ring that he'd slipped over his shaft before coming into the room. The ring held his erection tightly and prevented him from coming right on the spot. The cock cage as well as the cock ring also had a new state-of-the-art feature. Both would expand and grow with his cock if it became necessary, the erotic grip was rumored to allow him to keep a hard-on for as long as he needed without spewing or injury to his cock.

It was a great invention, allowing him peace of mind. He needed the time because he wanted to make love to Jenna until she was screaming and begging to join him in the Ménage Club and pleading to give their relationship another try with the help of a third.

As he heard a nearby door whisper open behind him, he couldn't stop himself from tensing. The next few minutes would be the most important part of tonight's Initiation. If they were to continue their relationship, now was the time for Jenna to face her worst fear.

Would she bolt? Or would she accept what was about to happen to him?

Jenna was thoroughly enjoying the sultry sensations of Tony's hands smoothing over her breasts, the slow, erotic tremors of the vibrator buried deep in her cunt and the gentle yet erotic pulse of the clit stimulator massaging her clitoris. Everything kept her aroused, sexually tense and on the edge.

The thing that turned her on the most, however, was the way Sully looked at her with a combination of such love and lust it made happiness hug her heart.

And then she detected movement behind him.

Noticed a pair of feminine arms clad in black fishnet curl over his shoulders, reaching for his nipples.

A tingle of uneasiness zapped through her as one of her worst fears was suddenly staring her right in the face.

Another woman had her hands on her man! And Sully appeared to be enjoying it!

She tried to calm the frantic beating of her heart as she watched. Whoever stood behind Sully, whoever was touching him so sensuously, tweaking his nipples until they became erect and red and hard, and had him moaning with arousal, wasn't showing herself.

Hurt slashed through her at the thought that someone else besides herself could bring out those sensual moans. But when she looked into his eyes and continued to see the love shining there just for her, despite another woman touching him, she began to feel something else nudge away her anger.

Anticipation.

A craving to join the woman in pleasuring Sully. She tried to get up, to break free of the bonds that held her wrists captive, but the soft binds only dug into her flesh, preventing her from going to him.

In response, Tony's hands simulated what the woman was doing to Sully. Pleasure-pain burst through her as he pinched her nipples. Perspiration dotted her forehead as the vibrator, as if sensing her increase in tension, began a mad pulse, effectively taking her thoughts off Sully and the woman, and back to her own sensations. The increased stimulation made her cry out, made her legs spread wider, her hips arch higher in anticipation. She hoped Sully would see her distress and come to her rescue by plunging his cock into her.

He didn't come.

She could tell he wanted to. Could see him move his wide chest against the woman's exploring hands, watched the woman holding him back.

She'd expected to feel hatred for the mysterious woman. Instead, she felt joy at the pleasure splashing across Sully's face. She expected to feel anger at Tony for not releasing her bonds and allowing her to go to her man, instead, she felt immense pleasure beneath his hands.

God! This Ménage Club sure knew what they were doing!

When the mysterious woman finally showed herself, Jenna exhaled a sign of relief. It was Meemee! And she'd changed from her flirty dress into a seamless, black fishnet, open-crotch body stocking that illuminated all her sexy feminine curves.

Despite her wanting not to feel anger toward her best friend at roving her hands over Sully, now that she knew the identity of the woman, Jenna felt the sharp blade of pain and betrayal slip through her. To her surprise, it wasn't as bad as she'd thought it would be.

She could handle this. She could handle whatever was coming next.

Chapter Six

SULLY COULD FEEL HIS need to get to Jenna growing as Meemee's seductive touches slipped downward. When her long, slender fingers gently cupped his rock-hard balls, he heard both himself and Jenna cry out.

He hadn't even realized he'd closed his eyes but, at the sound of her outcry, his eyes snapped open and he sucked in a hell of a sharp breath.

Tony had maneuvered himself between Jenna's legs. He'd removed the straps from the vibrator and was now plunging it slowly in and out of her tight slit.

Jenna's face was contorted in erotic bliss. The sight of her squirming beneath Tony's ministrations, unable to break from her bonds, made his breath come faster. The smell of her arousal made him swear softly.

Never in his life had he ever wanted a woman like he wanted to be with Jenna now.

As if sensing his need, Meemee's fingers wrapped tighter around his balls, holding him in place, preventing him from rushing to Jenna, preventing him from pushing Tony aside and plunging into her, bringing her the relief they both craved.

The look of mixed pleasure and desperation splashed on Sully's face tortured her, burned her with a need so deep she swore it shot straight into her very soul.

Although another woman was stroking his cock, making him swell and grow hard with arousal, he still kept looking at her, the lust and love mingling in his eyes. Lust and love for her!

She could see Sully's hands were clenched. Noticed he wasn't touching Meemee. Why not? Why was he refusing to bring Meemee any arousal?

Jenna watched the sensual way her best friend moved her fishnet-clad breasts against Sully's sinewy arms, the way her eyes were glazed over as she looked at Tony between Jenna's legs as he continued to plunge the vibrator into her.

Despite Sully's inattention, she could see Meemee was highly aroused.

Jenna held her breath as she watched Meemee's fingers grope Sully's rigid, captive cock. His flesh seemed a darker purple with the bondage gear. Even his eyes were a darker green than she'd ever seen before.

She whimpered through a growing sensual haze as Meemee's aroused gaze crashed into hers. They held eye contact for a moment and, within that short span of time, Jenna felt happiness, gratefulness and thankfulness that her friend would actually do something so extreme to help Jenna get over her jealous tenancies, helping Sully and her get back together. She also gave a silent thanks to the Ménage Club for being considerate enough of her fears in not throwing a perfect stranger at her and Sully during their first night there.

Best of all, no negative feelings lingered as she watched her best friend step to Sully's side. Meems brushed her curvy breast like a wanton hussy against Sully's muscular arm.

Meemee kept watching her. Gazing at her as if she were testing her to see if Jenna was angry or not at seeing Meemee with Sully.

When Meemee gave Tony a nod, Jenna felt the mattress move and realized she'd passed the test. At least this time.

She whimpered at the sensitivity in her breasts as Meemee left Sully and both she and Tony came to her sides, each latching their hot mouths onto her nipples.

Oh, God! She'd never felt anything like it. Pleasure coursed through her as their tongues swirled around her buds, their teeth nipped gently and suckled hard, making her just about climax on the spot.

She needed Sully between her legs now.

And she meant now! Wanted Sully whispering endearments into her ear. Thrusting his rigid cock into her. Telling her he loved her.

Through her erotic haze, she saw Sully come toward her.

She groaned at the sight of him.

Powerful. Strong. Magnificently aroused. And he wanted her!

She couldn't stop herself from whimpering. Couldn't stop the flames engulfing her as Sully came over her. His fingers wrapped around her ankles bringing her legs up and spreading them wide allowing her feet to dangle over his shoulders.

She cried out as he removed the soaked vibrator from her pussy. A moment later she felt the lubricated vibrator slip into her ass. It entered easily thanks to the self-lubricating feature Sully had mentioned and the state-of-the-art butt plug she'd worn for most of the last week in preparation for this night. The vibrator filled her anal canal with such heated pressure she couldn't help but blow out a breath. Sully wound the straps around her thighs, again holding the vibrator securely inside her. The item shivered to life, sending tremors of pleasure and pressure shimmering inside her.

Oh, God! That felt unbelievably good!

He didn't need to arouse her any further. It was as if he knew it.

With a wicked grin, his fingers sank into her thighs like heat-seeking missiles and he spread her legs wider, thrusting his large, thick cock into her in one swift plunge.

Magnificent explosions rattled her.

She screamed. Came apart.

As she cried out her release, Sully's immense thrusts became harder and, with Meemee and Tony's mouths sucking her nipples, Jenna could do nothing but rock with the pleasure.

His thrusting increased.

Sensations continued to spiral all around her.

She moaned.

Heard Sully groan.

Heard Tony groan also. Felt his mouth leave her breast. Heard a cry from Meemee as her friend's mouth left her other breast.

The mattress beside her began to move. She could hear Meemee whimper. Heard flesh slapping against flesh and assumed Tony was now fucking her best friend on the bed beside her.

As she came down from her climax, she could barely open her eyes, the sensual haze draped so heavily over her. Yet she was able to watch as Meemee, her fishnet-clad body on all fours, was being fucked by Tony.

God! What an erotic sight!

It only added to her pleasure and she rocked her hips as yet another climax gathered speed.

She trembled as she watched Sully. His eyes were mere slits, heavy with lust. His chest muscles heaved as both the vibrator and he continued to piston his delicious cock into both her openings, stuffing her as she'd never been filled before.

Her vagina tightened again, began to spasm. She couldn't keep the erotic sensations from coming.

And, boy, did they come.

She came again. Her mind shattered. Her body exploded in a carnal bliss that was even more powerful than the last orgasm.

She rode the magnificent waves.

Rode them hard.

From somewhere far away she heard Sully shout and felt his gush of release as he came inside her.

"WAKE UP, SLEEPYHEAD," The soft sound of Sully's voice made her grin. She loved it when he sounded so quiet and gentle. It was a direct contrast to the way he made love to her.

It was a wonderful combination. A combination she absolutely adored.

Stretching her sore limbs, she smiled at Sully Hero as he lay beside her on the bed watching her. There was no sight of Meemee or Tony. They were thankfully alone.

She needed to discuss what had just happened. Needed to tell him she'd enjoyed it immensely. Wondered if he had too.

"Was it as good for you as it was for me?" he asked. Reaching out, he skimmed a calloused finger along the side of her chin. Her skin tingled at his touch and she wanted more from him. Knew instinctively he wanted more too.

"I can't believe I've missed this sort of pleasure all these years," she admitted, reaching out to touch his firm lips. Lips meant for kissing, for suckling, biting.

He grinned and dragged her against him, kissing her mouth, possessing her, making her feel like she was his princess. His mate.

"Me neither," he breathed as he broke the intoxicating kiss.

"The pleasure can be yours for at least another year," Tony's voice drifted through the open bedroom doorway.

He was fully dressed. Wearing an expensive-looking pair of brown slacks and a Polo shirt, he looked quite serious. Meemee stood there also. Fully dressed in a pretty, flowery dress that enhanced all her feminine curves. It made her look really sharp, yet she had the same serious look on her face as Tony.

For a brief moment embarrassment flushed through her. Both Tony and Meemee had kissed her breasts, suckled her nipples. Her friend had watched as Tony had done intimate things to her.

Both had heard her cries of passion as Sully had made love to her.

However the embarrassment quickly dissipated as she told herself they were all perfectly healthy adults looking to help Sully and her get back together using unconventional means.

"As you know, Jenna, Sully came to the Ménage Club to ask us to help make your relationship last forever."

She snapped her gaze back to Sully, who smiled and nodded his head.

"The reason he did it was so he could not only get you back into his life but he also wants to learn how to keep you in his life and how to keep you happy. If you wish, we at the Ménage Club will proceed with both of you over the next year until you both are comfortable with your sex lives as well as the rest of your relationship."

Wow! Getting mind-blowing sex like she'd just experienced with Sully would be awesome. She'd never felt so good. So relaxed. So eager to be with him again.

Unfortunately, the excitement she felt didn't reflect on his face. He wore the same somber expression as Tony and Meemee.

Her tummy rolled. Obviously, what they were offering her was too good to be true.

"What's the catch?"

They all smiled and immediately her tenseness evaporated.

Tony held up some papers. "In my hand I have two contracts. One for you. One for Sully. What I am about to ask of you both will require an impulsive answer. There will be no time to discuss it amongst yourselves. Little time to think. Little time to react. Only time for a quick decision based on your primal instincts—instincts that will come straight from your hearts and not from your brains. This decision will be in effect for one year. This contract I am about to ask you to sign is what makes the Ménage Club 100% successful with bringing impossible relationships together."

"Gosh, you make it sound so serious," Jenna whispered, suddenly feeling the need to hold Sully's hand. It was as if he were thinking the same thing and intertwined his fingers with hers. She felt his power soar through her and knew instantly she could handle anything as long as she had Sully with her.

"What's the question?" Sully asked. His voice was a low whisper tinged with anxiety and hope.

"First, I will give you all the details. Each of you will be asked to sign a contract I am holding. As I mentioned, it will be in effect for one year. You will be asked to remain quiet about this club. Anything that is said here stays here. If you meet someone you feel may benefit from the Club, you do not automatically tell them about this Club nor do you invite them here. First, you must come to one of us and we will discuss it amongst ourselves and give you an answer. Is that understood?"

Both Jenna and Sully nodded.

"Good. Okay, the contract will be between each of you and the Ménage Club. If you sign these papers, then for one year you will come to the Club every night and experience what you've experienced here tonight. You will be required to pleasure each other with the help of a third and sometimes a fourth. Sometimes it will be me, sometimes it will be Meemee and then when you are both comfortable, others will also help. We at the Ménage Club each have our own specialties. You will experience them all...if you sign the contract. During the year, if either of you or both of you decide not to pursue your relationship, it will mean you have broken your contract as well as your mate's contract. This means dire consequences to both of you. It will be in both your interests to not break the contract once it is signed."

"What's in the contract, Tony?" Sully asked.

"If you and Jenna sign it, you will in effect be agreeing to what I've mentioned. Coming here for a few hours every evening. And I mean every evening. Days and the rest of the nights will belong to the both of you. You will do with that time what you wish. You can see each other or not see each other outside of Club hours. You can fight as much as you wish, but in the end, you must come to the Club and learn to pleasure each other and discuss your relationship and the reasons for your fights with the third and/or fourth assigned to you at that particular time. Statistics have proven that many fights and disagreements between couples have been worked out during their sex sessions. In your case, you will have a third with which to discuss any personal problems."

"Like our very own marriage counselor?" Jenna asked.

"Exactly," Tony agreed. "But before you agree, you must also realize you will face many challenges with a third. Questions will arise. Both of you will wonder if the third is a better lover than you are? Is he or she a better conversationalist? A better problem solver? These are just a few of the questions and insecurities. They are perfectly normal. Bring any problems you encounter immediately to light to your partner and with your third. Do not let it fester. You will be much better off in the long run. Trust will be learned and earned during this year. Pleasure will be learned. Our research has indicated that thrusting a third into your particular relationship will eventually allow you to trust each other. We gave you a taste of it tonight."

Making love to Sully every night didn't sound fatal. She could do that. She loved him. Had loved him for years. Wanted to learn to trust him. Yes, she would welcome counseling from a third in the bedroom and out. The Club had an unheard-of success rate. They couldn't lose.

"Do not answer me right this instant. You will be in separate rooms. Sully, I want you to go into the next room while Jenna makes her decision. Meemee will come with you and you will give her your decision. If you so choose to use the Club's resources you will sign the contract."

"What's in the contract?" she asked in a whisper.

"If either of you break the contract by leaving the other," Meemee said, "then, Sully, your bar is forfeited to the Ménage Club and, Jenna, you will forfeit your antiques shop to the Club as well."

Her tummy twisted as Sully frowned. She could feel his doubts intermingle with hers. Could they stay together for one year without breaking it off?

"You cannot discuss it with each other. Do you trust one another enough to sign these contracts? If not, you will not be given a second chance to join. Sully and Meemee, leave the room now."

Before he let go of her hand, Sully squeezed her fingers. Was it a squeeze of reassurance?

Sweet heavens! Could either of them make such a huge decision based on impulse and instincts? It was insane, wasn't it?

She tried to read Sully's expression, but couldn't. His face remained blank, as if he were deep in thought. He stood slowly, grabbed his robe and slipped into it, concealing the gorgeous muscles in his ass from her.

The instant the door closed behind him, Tony asked her the dreaded question.

"What is your answer?"

"Yes," Jenna whispered. Yes, she would risk her heart for another chance with Sully. But would he do the same?

"Sign on the dotted line then. If Sully decides not to join, both contracts are null and void. Is that understood?"

She nodded and the click of a pen quickly followed.

With an oddly steady hand, which surprised her, Jenna signed the contract. For some strange reason, she thought the contract would place a heavy weight on her. It didn't. Actually, it set her free. The Ménage Club would give her the hope and the trust she needed to be with Sully forever.

She had to trust he would want the same thing. She had to trust what he'd said earlier that the reason he had come back home was to be with her.

She giggled as she handed back the paper to Tony.

"Welcome to the Ménage Club, Jenna. We'll work hard with you to keep our success rating."

She nodded as she watched him leave and held her breath as she waited to hear Sully's answer.

"AND WHAT IS THE PRIZE when we make the year?" Sully asked Meemee as he quickly signed the contract. Instincts had told him Jenna would sign too. She loved him and he loved her. They just needed a little bit of time getting back on track.

"Do we get to own Ménage Club?" Sully asked jokingly as he handed the contract back to Meemee.

"Close. You will become part owners of the Club, yes. You will be allowed the privileges of ménages whenever you wish and know you are experiencing it in a safe environment. You may also, if you wish, participate in helping other couples in need such as yourselves, that is, if you don't break the contract."

"We won't break the contract," Jenna said as she entered the room where he'd been sequestered. She'd put that sexy white chemise on again and he couldn't wait to get her out of it.

"With the Ménage Club behind us we're going to make it," she said softly, her gorgeous blue eyes sparkled with happiness.

Yes, they would make it, of that he was sure.

"And on the odd chance you don't make it, we will take your businesses away from you and they will be sold—the money goes to a charity of your choice," Tony replied as he strolled into the room.

"Hmm, that's a noble cause. Maybe we should break up right now?" Sully teased as he reached out to Jenna, pulling her onto his lap.

She smiled warmly and melted against him like a cat. Her sweet scent swarmed all around him, making him hard again, making him want to cuddle her, be intimate with her and talk about their future.

"And give up a year of ménages...with you? No way, Sully Hero. You answered my ad and now that I have you I'm never letting you go."

"I do love the sound of that, Jenna MacLean. And I know it won't be easy regaining your trust but, I promise, you'll have a lot of fun practicing trusting me again."

In answer she nipped sharply at his chin and curled her arms around his neck, her eyes smiling mischievously.

"Then let's get practicing."

The End

~ Pleasure Bound Series ~

On the planet of Paradise, in the not-so-distant future, women rule and men are slaves. But three male astronauts and their three sisters are going to shake things up!

A Hero's Welcome - Book One

A Hero Escapes - Book Two

A Hero Betrayed - Book Three

A Hero's Kiss - Book Four

A Hero Wanted - Book Five

Captive Heroes - Book Six

Also available in the Pleasure Bound Complete Series Boxed Set!

A Hero's Welcome - Book One

BEING INJURED AND HELD captive isn't what astronaut Joe Hero had in mind when he agreed to explore a newly discovered planet for NASA. But a man would have to be dead not to fall for the sexy female doctor in charge of his care.

One night of scorching passion in the arms of the stranger from another planet is enough to convince Annie that there's much more to males than she's been taught. Who is this sexy hunk and why does she feel like welcoming him into her bed every chance she gets?

A Hero's Welcome takes place on a planet far away from Earth. Their ways are different than ours. There is some bdsm and erotica in this series. Reader discretion is advised.

A Hero Escapes - Book Two

QUEEN JACEY HAS ALWAYS fantasized about bedding a male. But taking one for her enjoyment is strictly forbidden on her planet. That is, until an attractive stranger from another planet makes her to overcome her training and her beliefs. Being held captive and mating with a gorgeous Queen isn't exactly what astronaut Ben Hero expected when he agreed to explore a newly discovered planet for NASA. Escaping should be his top priority but making sizzling love to Jacey is all he can think about. When he discovers they are both prisoners, Ben's protective instincts kick in big time.

Suddenly they're on the run, irresistibly aroused, and wrapped in each other's arms every chance they get!

Please note: A Hero Escapes is a futuristic erotic romance fiction and takes place on a planet far away from Earth. Their ways are much different than ours. Readers sensitive to erotica bdsm, bondage and a Queen's forbidden fantasy coming true, should not purchase this book.

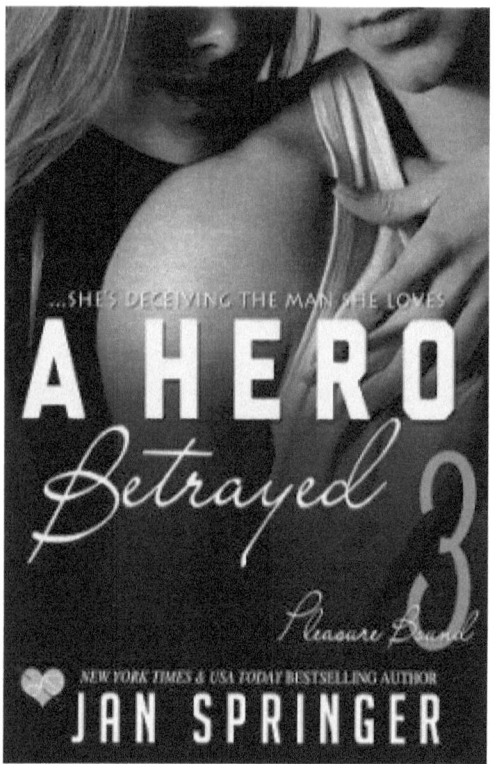

A Hero Betrayed - Book Three

ASTRONAUT BUCK HERO didn't count on being held captive or becoming infected with passion poison when he agreed to explore a newly discovered planet for NASA. If he doesn't get the cure soon he's going to be one very dead man.

Fugitive on-the-run Virgin has just rescued an infected male and needs to administer the naughty cure - a twenty-four-hour making love marathon. Then she'll turn him over to his enemies in order to gain her freedom. But her well-laid plans go into orbit when she discovers she's fallen in love with the sexy stranger from another world.

A Hero Betrayed takes place on a planet far away from Earth. Their ways are different than ours. Some bdsm and erotica scenes are in this series. Reader Discretion is advised.

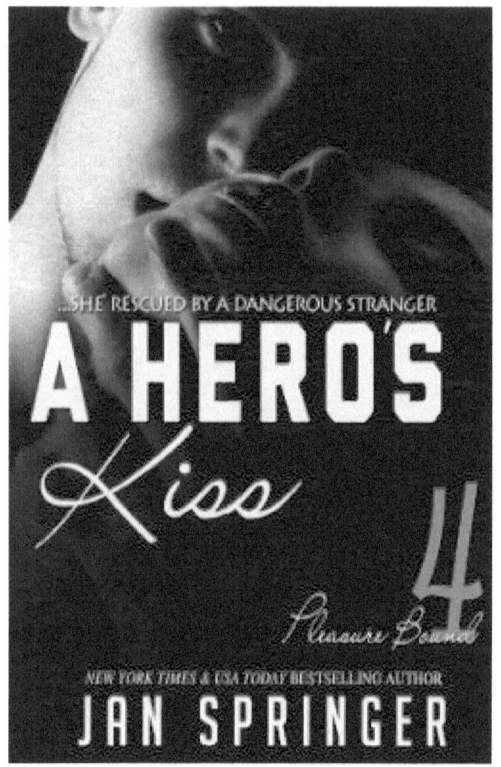

A Hero's Kiss - Book Four

ON A MISSION IN SEARCH of their missing brothers, US Astronaut Piper Hero and her two sisters become separated after crash-landing on a newly discovered planet...

Being injured and infected by sensuous swamp water isn't what Piper Hero signed up for when she agreed to search for her three missing brothers. But when she's rescued by a dangerously sexy man who makes her so hot that she can't even think straight, Piper is glad that she came.

Jarod Ellis has sworn off women. But he's captivated by Piper Hero, a woman who claims to be related to the Earthmen he has vowed to protect with his life. Although he mistrusts her, she sets free a carnal inferno of needs he's never experienced during his previous life as a pleasure slave.

A Hero's Kiss is Book 4 in the series and takes place on a planet far away from Earth. Their ways are different than ours. Some scenes in this series include bondage, voyeurism and erotica. Reader Discretion is advised.

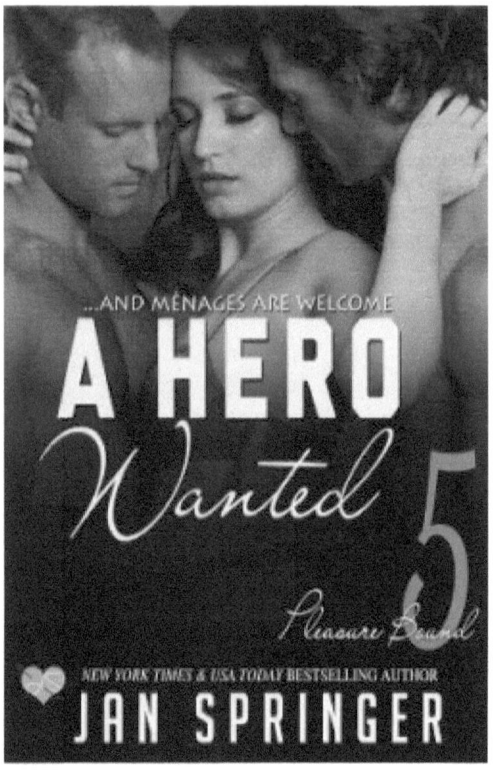

A Hero Wanted - Book Five

A HERO IS WANTED FOR plus-sized Jenna MacLean who is finally able to explore her most intimate side...and in her new world ménages are welcome.

"Old-fashioned girl needs a man who loves to walk in the rain. A homebody, white picket fence-type of guy. Sexual requirements-gentle yet untamed lover. He must be sexually adventurous who will train me to be the same. Must be romantic, enjoy toys, interested in mutual light bondage, ménages are welcome."

That's what curvy, antiques shop owner Jenna MacLean wants when she and her best friend outline a want ad just for fun on their weekly girls' night out.

After years of being away from his pretty-plus sized ex-girlfriend, Sully's back in town. When he finds the want ad, he knows he's the only man who can make all of Jenna's sizzling-hot fantasies come true. She's never left his heart and he needs her back in his bed-but he's not going to get her back via the traditional romantic route. This time, he'll prove he loves her with help from the notorious Ménage Club, a relationship club designed specifically to get estranged couples back together with the help of a third and sometimes a fourth in the bedroom...

Captive Heroes - Book Six

During a secret NASA mission to locate their brothers on the faraway planet of Paradise, the Hero sisters become separated after they crash land...and find unexpected romance with the tormented alien male warriors of the species in this ultra-long scifi book that completes the Pleasure Bound series.

Taylor and Kayla

While searching for her brothers, Kayla Hero is bound and imprisoned by the Breeders— along with a male captive whose tantalizing scars pique her interest. Forced to escape with him, she's irresistibly aroused when she suddenly becomes his captive.

Wild lust flares in Kayla's eyes— a sensual side effect of the Fever Swamp water she's accidentally ingested. Taylor knows he will enjoy administering the cure — lots of sizzling hot lovemaking!

Blackie and Kinley

Injured and lost in a dense jungle, Kinley Hero is intimidated by the scarred man who hunts her, especially due to the power of erotic submission he holds over her.

Capturing his beautiful female prey, Blackie can't wait to train her as a pleasure slave for the Death Valley Boys. When her captor slips a collar around her neck, Kinley must struggle with lust as a natural submissive.

~ Pleasure Bound Series ~

A Hero's Welcome - Book One
A Hero Escapes - Book Two
A Hero Betrayed - Book Three
A Hero's Kiss - Book Four
A Hero Wanted - Book Five
(Book Five is loosely connected to the series)
Captive Heroes - Book Six

Want more Jan Springer Adult Romances?
Mini Catalog
Kidnap Fantasies Series
In the land of the rich and famous, the top-secret Kidnap Fantasies is
the answer to discreet and naughty downtime.

Book One
Jade's Fantasy
When ex-downhill skier Jade's two sisters give her a Kidnap Fantasies
questionnaire, Jade is aroused at the prospect of having no-strings fun
in the sun with a stranger whose only job would be to fulfill her every
intimate fantasy. Although she knows she's too shy to send it in, she
secretly pours her deepest wishes into the questionnaire.
Soon the questionnaire mysteriously vanishes and Jade's fantasy man
appears on her luxury yacht in the form of a sexy handy man who gives
her an intimate toy-filled holiday she'll never forget.

Book Two
Christmas Lovers
(can also be found in the Merry Ménage Kisses Boxed Set)
Sergeant Connor Jordan, wounded overseas and sent back to the
States to recuperate, just cannot stop fantasizing about the sexy nurse
who cared for him. When his brothers give him a holiday gift
certificate to Kidnap Fantasies, a top-secret fantasy organization,
Connor knows he'll use their gift, if only to help him forget his
wickedly delicious attraction to Nurse Sparks.
Nurse Tania Sparks has always been purely professional with her
injured soldiers...until sinfully sexy Connor Jordan enters her hospital.
He makes her body throb with an intense desire she's never known
before. The last thing she wants is to get involved with the injured
warrior. So what's a woman supposed to do to relieve her naughty
frustrations? Call Kidnap Fantasies and have them supply her with a
look-alike man who'll help her forget her sexy soldier...

When Tania and Connor unexpectedly come together at a secluded mountain chalet, their love explodes in a ménage of passion, sensuous desires and a happily forever after.

Contains ménage scenes.

Book Three
Zero to Sexy

Because Santana hides from something bad in his past he lives only for the moment and doesn't dare dream of a future. He exists within the sensual world of Kidnap Fantasies, a top-secret escort world where he explores his sexuality and enjoys pleasure with both men and women. But it is love at first sight the instant he sees Amy at his good friend's wedding. She's got future written all over her. He knows she is a hunger he must deny, so why is he whispering "you're mine" to her at the wedding?

The instant Amy Sparks sees the handsome African American at her sister's wedding, she knows in her heart that he's everything she's ever fantasized about in a lover, but before they can connect, he mysteriously disappears. Upon discovering he works for Kidnap Fantasies, she knows how he'll make all her intimate fantasies come true...

When Santana's next Kidnap Fantasies assignment turns out to be Amy, he knows he must protect her from his past and he can be with her only this one time...

Reader Advisory: Includes a sizzling ménage scene and some male on male sensual interaction.

Boxed Sets

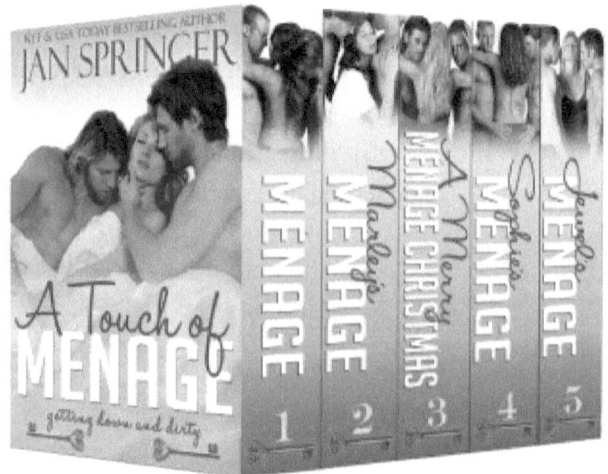

SIX Erotic Romance Ménage Stories! INCLUDES A BONUS MÉNAGE EBOOK

Step into The Key Club's Ménage Nights where naughty fantasies come true and two men are hotter than one. Includes FIVE bestselling The Key Club stories; Ménage, Marley's Ménage, A Merry Ménage Christmas, Sophie's Ménage and Jewel's Ménage.

She's getting three...

Cowboys
FOR
Christmas

A Cowboys Online Novel

JAN SPRINGER

NEW YORK TIMES & USA TODAY
BESTSELLING AUTHOR

BONUS Ménage BOOK "Cowboys for Christmas" book 1 of Jan's new Cowboys Online series. Jennifer Jane is getting THREE Cowboys for Christmas ~ What more could a girl want?

Jennifer Jane Watson has spent the past ten Christmases in a maximum-security prison. The last thing she expects is to get early parole along with a job on a secluded Canadian cattle ranch serving Christmas holiday dinners to three of the sexiest cowboys she's ever met!

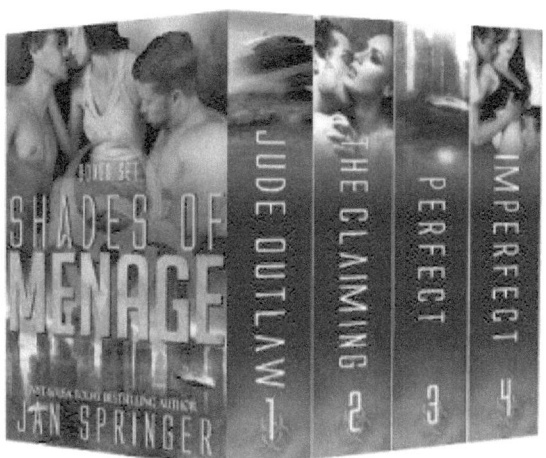

Shades of Ménage Boxed Set: Four Book Romance Ménage Collection

A fast-acting virus has killed a majority of the world's female population. Women's rights are stripped away and The Claiming Law is created, allowing groups of men to stake a claim on a female—as their sensual property.

After five years of fighting in the Terrorist Wars, the Outlaw brothers are coming home to declare ownership on the women they love...and they'll do it any way they can in **Jude Outlaw and The Claiming**.

PLUS

In the future...for population control, each human is embedded with a microchip that suppresses the urge to mate.

*Centuries later,...*A rebel group of young doctors are secretly tampering with their microchips and experimenting with intimacy. Now they search for allies who can help them with their cause – to eventually free humanity in the Dystopian Romance Ménage stories **"Perfect"** & **"Imperfect"**.

A CONTEMPORARY EROTIC ROMANCE BOXED SET
Naughty Girl Desires Boxed Set: Romance, Contemporary Romance, Romance Suspense, Box Set
(m/f only)

What You'll Find Inside Naughty Girl Desires
Jade's Fantasy
Kidnap Fantasies 1
Jan Springer

In the land of the rich and famous, Kidnap Fantasies is the answer to discreet naughty downtime.

When ex-downhill skier Jade Hart's two sisters give her a Kidnap Fantasies questionnaire, Jade is aroused at the prospect of having no-strings fun in the sun with a stranger whose only job would be to fulfill her every intimate fantasy. Although she knows she's too shy to send it in, she secretly pours her deepest wishes into the questionnaire. Soon the questionnaire mysteriously vanishes and Jade's fantasy man appears on her luxury yacht in the form of a sexy handy man who gives her an intimate toy-filled Christmas holiday she'll never forget.

The Biker and The Bride
Jan Springer

Wrapped in red-hot lust for revenge, Avery plots to murder the man responsible for the death of her son. Her plans are dashed when her ex-husband crashes her wedding and whisks her away on his motorcycle to the rustic Canadian wilderness cabin they'd once honeymooned.

Police detective, Mason is fighting for Avery's love with everything he has.

Armed with whipped cream, handcuffs and his undying devotion, Mason vows he will make Avery love again. But it's only a matter of time before the man she'd planned to kill hunts them down...

Sinderella Sexy
Jan Springer

By day, she's a dedicated gynecologist.
By night, Dr. Ella Cinder, escapes reality by secretly performing in her own erotic, adult version of Cinderella, aptly re-titled Sinderella.
When sexy colleague Dr. Roarke Stephenson shows up in the Sinderella audience on the same night her Prince Charming stands her up, Ella seizes the opportunity to make Roarke into her Prince

Charming for one carnal night of extremely naughty fun in front of an audience.

But at the strike of midnight, Ella knows she must face the harsh reality that Roarke must never learn her secret life and they can never be together again. Until then, she'll make sure he'll never forget their night of sensual play.

Dr. Roarke Stephenson is immediately captured by the lusciously curvy actress who hides behind a mask and is known only as Sinderella. For some insane reason she reminds him of his klutzy co-worker, Ella. But that's not possible. Ella would never have the nerve to do the wickedly delicious things Sinderella does to him, or would she?

Nice Girl Naughty
Jan Springer

Blind since nineteen, Summer has blossomed into a famous wood carver. When she's almost killed by a serial killer, she's whisked away to a secluded wilderness cabin by the man she once secretly loved. Summer can't get enough of touching professional bodyguard Nick Cassidy's thick, powerful muscles and all those other hard, yummy male body parts that she has always longed to explore.

For years Nick has stayed away from his best friend's kid sister, nice girl Summer. Now he's back, and sweeping his gorgeous redhead into the naughty cravings he's always had for her. With passion blinding him, Nick doesn't realize their hideout isn't safe—until it's too late.

**For more Jan Springer stories, please visit
http://www.janspringer.com**

Jan's Newsletter

Hi! If you would like to get an email when my books are released, you
can sign up here:

Newsletter: http://ymlp.com/xguembmugmgb

Your emails will never be shared and you can unsubscribe whenever
you like.

For newsletters regarding foreign translated Jan Springer ebooks and
print books: https://janspringerauthor.wordpress.com/newsletters/

About the Author

Jan Springer writes full-time at her home nestled in cottage country, Ontario, Canada. She enjoys hiking, kayaking, gardening, reading and writing. She is a member of the Writers Union of Canada, Romance Writers of America. She loves hearing from her readers.

A Word From The Author

Hi! Thank you for purchasing this book. Word of mouth is important for any author to succeed. If you enjoyed this story feel free to leave a short review at the place where you bought it. I would really appreciate it. I look forward to bringing you more stories in the near future. Thanks!

If you would like to contact me or personally send me feedback, you can reach me by using my contact page at:

http://janspringerauthor.wordpress.com/contact/

Here are other ways we can connect:
Jan Springer Website at http://www.janspringer.com
Instagram – http://www.instagram.com/janspringerauthor
Facebook - https://www.facebook.com/janspringereroticromance
Twitter - https://twitter.com/janspringer @janspringer
Pinterest - http://www.pinterest.com/janspringer1/
Jan's Blog - http://janspringerauthor.wordpress.com/blog-2/
LinkedIn - http://ca.linkedin.com/in/janspringerauthor/
Google Plus - https://plus.google.com/u/0/
101527334949931513035/posts
Jan's Newsletter - http://ymlp.com/xguembmugmgb
Goodreads - https://www.goodreads.com/author/show/
260628.Jan_Springer
Happy Reading,
jan springer

Don't miss out!

Visit the website below and you can sign up to receive emails whenever Jan Springer publishes a new book. There's no charge and no obligation.

https://books2read.com/r/B-A-WGQ-IXDI

BOOKS 2 READ

Connecting independent readers to independent writers.